Praise for Linda Olsson

"Linda Olsson's [*Astrid & Veronika*] casts the themes of secrecy, passion, and loss in the shape of a double helix, intertwining the stories of two women . . . Natural and vivid, utterly convincing . . . simply so beguiling."
　　—*The New York Times Book Review*

"Linda Olsson evokes, with great precision and beauty, the landscape of a friendship . . . *Astrid & Veronika* is penetrating and beautifully written, and it affirms the power of narrative to transform."
　　—Kim Edwards, author of
　　　The Memory Keeper's Daughter

"Readers of Anne Tyler and Jodi Picoult will appreciate the lyrical prose and expert rendering of the themes of heartbreak and loss."
　　—*Booklist*

"Olsson's deft writing [is] beautiful, capable of both painting the scene and creating a mood . . . Booksellers from around the country as well as locally have raved about *Astrid & Veronika*. It's easy to understand why."
　　—*Portland Tribune*

"[*Astrid & Veronika*] has the hallmarks of an Ingmar Bergman film: a leisurely pace, a chilly Scandinavian setting leavened by rich observations of nature, and characters whose prim, polite facades eventually disappear, exposing years of anger and hurt."

—*Kirkus Reviews*

"Olsson understands how memory works—the combination of fact and fiction, photographs and moments . . . Readers will love [*Sonata for Miriam*]."

—*Los Angeles Times Book Review*

"Olsson's eloquent prose [in *The Memory of Love*] offers an intimate, poignant portrait of a woman at midlife who finds her way back . . . to a life filled with love."

—*Publishers Weekly*

PENGUIN BOOKS

A SISTER IN MY HOUSE

LINDA OLSSON was born in Stockholm, Sweden, in 1948. She graduated from Stockholm University with a law degree and worked in law and finance until she left Sweden in 1986. What was intended as a three-year posting to Kenya then became a tour of the world with stops in Singapore, the UK, and Japan, until she settled in New Zealand with her family in 1990. In 1993 she completed a bachelor of arts in English and German literature at Victoria University of Wellington. Her first novel, *Astrid & Veronika*, became an international success. It was followed by *Sonata for Miriam* and *The Memory of Love*. Olsson divides her time between Auckland, New Zealand, and Stockholm, Sweden.

A SISTER
IN MY
HOUSE

A NOVEL

LINDA OLSSON

PENGUIN BOOKS

PENGUIN BOOKS

An imprint of Penguin Random House LLC
375 Hudson Street
New York, New York 10014
penguin.com

Originally published in Swedish as *En syster i mitt hus*
by Brombergs Bokförlag, Stockholm.

LIBRARY OF CONGRESS CATALOGING-IN-PUBLICATION DATA

Names: Olsson, Linda, author.
Title: A sister in my house : a novel / Linda Olsson.
Other titles: Syster i mitt hus. English
Description: New York : Penguin Books, 2018
Identifiers: LCCN 2017016917 | ISBN 9780143131694 (pbk.)
| ISBN 9781524705565 (ebook)
Classification: LCC PT9877.25.L77 S9713 2018 | DDC 839.73/8—dc23
LC record available at https://lccn.loc.gov/2017016917

Printed in the United States of America
1   3   5   7   9   10   8   6   4   2

Set in Aldus LT STD   ·   Designed by Elke Sigal

To Sally, with gratitude for Hatepe

One Sister have I in our house—
And one, a hedge away.
There's only one recorded,
But both belong to me.

—EMILY DICKINSON

A SISTER IN MY HOUSE

I can't explain why I did it. Often, it is as if a part of me has its own impulsive life beyond my control. I am astounded at the mess it causes. And occasionally at the good that comes of it regardless. But whichever way, it is always my conscious self that has to deal with the consequences. Good or bad.

Now, when I look back at how this particular whim came to have such a profound effect on how I view myself and my life, I can't understand that I had no notion of it at the time. That I didn't understand the seriousness of my ill-considered invitation. A few words sprung from some cache deep inside me, seemingly without any particular effect when uttered. None that I was able to discern at the time, anyway.

Was there perhaps some subconscious intention? Some unacknowledged hope that lingered deep inside me? Was I after all affected by what had preceded that moment when I stood facing my sister and invited her to come visit me?

Or was there something about her that caused me to speak those words? I don't know. I can't answer my own questions. I don't understand myself.

All I can do is accept the consequences. And try to live the rest of my life as best I can. Try to savor what remains of what I previously so lightly discarded.

DAY ONE

"Which bed shall I make for the guest?" asked the young woman who stood facing me in the semidark dining room. Her brown eyes were expressionless. To her, it was just a practical question, of course.

But the words struck me as if I had swallowed something hot and heavy. And once ingested, they came to rest somewhere deep inside me, burning. The realization that when evening arrived, my sister would be here. Sleep in one of the beds. Occupy one of the rooms. Invade the space I considered mine. And affect the atmosphere. Not because of some intention on her part. No, it was me. I was the problem. What I consider mine has always felt so very . . . I am not sure how to describe it. Fragile perhaps. So exposed and vulnerable. In every way. I am unable to share anything that truly means something to me. And when circumstances force me to, all I want to do is walk away. Leave everything behind. It is forever ruined for me. When I think about it, I see it has always been like that. Before Emma existed too. Perhaps I am so afraid of losing, if I put up a fight, that I give up without even trying. It is not something I am proud of, but now I am able to acknowledge, without any sense of shame or guilt, that this is how it is.

I swallowed hard, to no effect. The heat had reached my stomach and I felt nauseous. The young woman waited patiently for my response. My thoughts flew from the master bedroom behind me, down the stairs, to the two bedrooms in the basement. That was where I wanted to place my sister. But if I didn't sleep in the master bedroom myself, wouldn't it seem strange not to give it to her? On the other hand, letting her have it would mean giving her a larger part of the house than I wanted to. Not just because it was the largest room but also because of its position on the entrance floor, at the heart of the house. It would be like giving her access to more of my house than I liked to. It felt as if she were already here and already affecting my relationship with the house. The nausea kept rising.

"The first room downstairs, I think," I said to the girl, and she nodded and disappeared down the stairs.

I slowly walked upstairs, to the top floor. The space there was one room, a large open area where indoors and outdoors was separated only by a glass wall with sliding doors. With the doors open, you would feel as if you were outside, and often small birds would come to visit. I spent most of my time up there. I slept on one of the hard sofas. I ate out on the terrace, unless it rained. And I worked there. It was a large house, and I really only occupied the top part of it. But I liked the feeling of the rest of it being there, below me. It worked like a kind of buffer against the world.

I walked out onto the terrace, which I used to think of as my garden. The first one I'd ever had. But it was really just a space with terra-cotta tiles on the floor and a few potted plants. A lemon tree, a lime, a vine that grew slowly, supported by the stone wall, and a few red and pink geraniums. The large, mature bougainvillea didn't quite belong, I thought, although it filled the entire left part of the terrace with its purple splendor. It had its roots beneath the flagstones in the street below, and I never considered it my responsibility. How it had grown to such height and width was a mystery. Its extravagant blossoms overshadowed the modest efforts of the other plants. I never watered it, but it didn't seem to matter. It must have found its own source of nourishment somewhere deep below.

I looked up to the sky and raised my hand to count the number of fingers between the sun and the ridge of the hills. At least an hour of daylight left. That would make it around five thirty, and the bus wasn't due until just after eight. I had time to finish the day's gardening if I got on with it straightaway. Water the plants, pick up dry leaves and twigs, sweep the floor, and fold the sun chairs. But I remained seated.

I heard the girl call good-bye from downstairs, then the sound of the front door opening and closing, followed by the gate to the alleyway, and finally the sound of her rapid, light steps on the street below.

The house was mine again.

I stood up and went downstairs. The kitchen appeared very dark after the intense light on the terrace. I poured myself a glass of cold white wine and brought it with me upstairs.

It wasn't just the plants on the terrace that needed care; the house itself also felt like a living organism that needed me. Or perhaps it was I who needed the house. It embraced me and protected me. It seemed to strive toward the sun, just like the plants did. And perhaps that was why I too lived up there, close to the sun. Far below, where the bougainvillea had its roots, were the bedrooms, always cool and in semi-darkness, even when I opened the shutters. The kitchen and dining room on the entrance floor also stayed cool, even in the summer, and I found this comforting somehow. It was hard to imagine what it would feel like in the winter.

Ever since I'd first arrived, I'd slept with the curtains open. I learned how to determine the time of day with only a quick glance. I liked that and by now I trusted my assessment of the light more than I had ever trusted a watch.

I saw the most beautiful sunrises and night skies of my life, and I never tired of gazing out over the bay below, where the surface of the sea constantly shifted color and mood. The white buildings climbed up the slope from the harbor, forming a kind of amphitheater, and beyond them the crest of the steep hills constituted a protective wall. I loved the view the most like this, at the end of the day.

This would be my first complete year in the house. My first winter. I no longer had any other home, although I wasn't sure I could count on being allowed to renew the lease at the end of the year or would be able to buy the house. But I thought no further than the end of the year. Wood was stacked by the fireplace in the dining room, so I assumed it might get cold eventually. But the sea was still swimmable and the sun warm.

I sat down on the wooden bench at the table and took a sip of wine. I drank too much. Too much in comparison to what? I twirled the glass in my hand and watched the condensation become tears that fell on my fingers. There wasn't really any need for me to compare myself with anything or anybody. As long as I was alone in the house, all comparisons were meaningless. Here there were no rules or regulations. Whether I drank too much could only be measured by how I felt. And apart from the hot knot in my stomach, I felt fine. This too without comparison. Fine for me. Fine for now.

I put the glass down and placed my hands on either side

of it. They were strong hands, though not exactly beautiful. I hadn't been given the long, narrow fingers with beautifully shaped nails or, for that matter, the attractive slim legs. Or those dainty feet. Or the blonde hair. Strangely, this had never bothered me. Rather the opposite, really. I couldn't remember ever having wanted it to be different. I realized that Emma had inherited Mother's beauty, of course. That ethereal quality. The self-evident femininity. An attractive fragility, perhaps also a kind of vulnerability. I honestly couldn't recall ever having envied her anything in that respect.

But, then, initially I wasn't alone. Then, when I had Amanda, I saw my reflection in Amanda and I liked what I saw.

Emma could keep her beauty.

Abruptly, I felt the anxiety rise again. Anxiety? No, it was more than that. It was dread. Panic really. I quickly took a large sip of wine. Perhaps I ought to take a shower? Change into something fresh? I looked down at the striped cotton dress I was wearing. It had been a long time since I had ironed my clothes. Just as I dropped many other chores and routines. Peeled away most of them. No, that wasn't really what had happened. It hadn't been a conscious decision. Rather, there had been a time when even the simplest practical chore had felt completely overwhelming. And that was when I abandoned most things. And lost a hold on my life.

I felt a small stab of something I couldn't quite define. Grief perhaps? Or bitterness? I hoped it wasn't the latter. Grief was acceptable. That old, inexhaustible grief that survived inside me. I could live with that. I might even need it in order to survive. Then, on top of it, the newer, not-yet-set grief. I nurtured that one. But bitterness has always scared me. I inspected my nails again and realized I couldn't even remember when I had last painted them. Or when I had worn makeup. I cut my own hair and usually wore it held back with a clasp. Now I removed the clasp and shook out my hair. A shower, definitely.

There was still plenty of time.

I stood under the lukewarm water, with my eyes closed. I knew exactly when it had seized me, this mad impulse. I could see us standing there, Emma and I. A few stray guests lingered, but the reception was over.

The two of us, as if inside a bubble. It felt strange. I had never experienced a sense of belonging with Emma. Not even when we were children. But I remember that I stopped in my tracks, a pile of dirty dishes in my hands, and looked at her.

"Would you like to come and visit, Emma? Stay with me in my house in Spain?"

She threw me a quick glance, with those large, pale eyes of hers a little red on the rims. She looked surprised, but she made no immediate response, just carried on picking up cutlery and scrunched napkins from the table. When her hands were full, she turned and disappeared into the kitchen.

"It would be nice if you'd come," I said when she returned, trying to make it sound as if I didn't really care too much either way. But there was something inside me that just had to say it, regardless. I do remember that I regretted the words as soon as they passed my lips.

"Oh, I don't know, Maria," she said eventually, without looking up.

I shrugged, as if it made no difference whatsoever to me. And I realized I was relieved.

"It's just a bit much right now . . ." She left the sentence unfinished. "Perhaps later. If the invitation still stands. Sometime later."

"Later" became almost two years. And by then I had forgotten my strange impulse. So much had happened in the interim. Now as I tried to think back and understand why I had blurted out that invitation, I reluctantly had to acknowledge that I might have been driven by a wish to show off. To flaunt my new life. Strut my happiness.

Mother always used to say that you mustn't allow yourself to be happy. Or at least not admit it, not to yourself. And certainly not to other people. Never show it. To do that is to challenge the powers and inevitably leads to catastrophe. If that is true, Mother must certainly have been safe. I can't remember ever seeing her happy. As for me, in spite of not really wanting to, I became cautious too.

Somehow it became ingrained in me. But right at that moment, then, when I stood facing Emma after Mother's funeral, strangely, I was happy. And for a moment I allowed myself to acknowledge that I was. Mother would be proven right, of course.

⚜

Emma was visibly affected by the occasion. She cried through the entire funeral ceremony. And now, as she bent forward and continued to collect plates and glasses from the table, I noticed tears falling again. I had not cried at all. I was comfortably cocooned in my happiness. Not because Mother was dead, but because of the future I so arrogantly took for granted.

The funeral wasn't a particularly shattering one. Mother's death was no surprise. We had been given time to prepare, and everything had been done exactly in accordance with Mother's wishes. Lots of music, the kind she liked. French chansons well performed by a young singer and a man with an accordion. But it was a celebration that should have happened earlier. And under other circumstances. Before the guest of honor had disappeared. As it was, it felt like an empty gesture, meaningless and a little awkward. We all played our parts, particularly Emma and I. With Mother hovering over us. Emma beautiful and suitably sad. I remember reflecting that she was in her element at the funeral. She mingled with the guests with the just the right amount of restrained grief. She had been born with that natural elegance about her. At home, elegance had certainly not been nurtured. Not much else either. You had what you were born with. Anything further, you had to find on your own elsewhere. Or manage without.

I turned off the water and stepped onto the cool, polished concrete floor and dried myself slowly and carefully. Even though I hadn't gained weight, and I really didn't think I had, it was as if the flesh was in a process of slow redistribution. I stood facing the mirror and stretched, straightened my back, and pulled in my chin. I had just turned forty-eight. All I could be certain of was that aging would progress, presumably at an increasing pace. As long as I refrained from comparing myself to my young self, or to someone else, the process could be allowed its course.

But then there was Emma.

I lifted first one arm, then the other, and regarded myself in the mirror. It felt as if it had been a long time since I had. And it felt as if the distance between me and my image had increased, as if we were slowly separating. I applied deodorant. Brushed my teeth. Why, I have no idea. I was soon to have another glass of wine. I combed my hair and quickly pulled on clean clothes. Jeans and a striped shirt. Then I took a step back and watched myself. And I realized that there I was, doing exactly what I shouldn't. I compared myself. To my younger self. To Mother. And foremost to Emma. She was forty-two. Six years younger than me.

It had seemed a big difference when Emma first entered my life. Then, as we grew older, it hadn't seemed much at all. Now, suddenly, it again felt like a considerable difference.

Six years earlier I had been happy.

I had heard nothing from Emma after the funeral. Not that I had expected it. I hadn't been in touch either. Our contact had always been sporadic, at best. Even during the last few months of Mother's life, I had not called very often. And when Emma and I talked, it rarely developed into a proper conversation. I asked what I thought I should ask. Extended offers to help financially. Offers that were nevertheless never taken up. Somehow it felt like Mother's illness was Emma's responsibility and only hers. Whether this was what I made myself believe because I felt guilty or was a fact, I am not sure. Emma never complained, never asked for anything. I think I was relieved. What little contact we had during those last few months before the funeral ceased completely afterward. It wasn't that Mother had been a link that held us together, exactly, but her physical presence might have provided a tangible reminder that we were related. Afterward, there was nothing left, and I hardly gave a thought to my sister or her life.

So Emma's e-mail arrived as a complete surprise.

Maria, I am not sure if you remember that you invited
me to visit you in Spain. If the invitation still stands, I
would very much like to come. Would sometime in
October suit?
        E

That was all. But it was just right. If she had written
more, asked about my health or added a greeting of some
kind, I would have reacted differently and probably not in
a good way. This short, neutral message was manageable.
It felt genuine and therefore difficult to dismiss. So I replied, yes, that would be just fine. Anytime in October.

Now it was the fourteenth. And Emma was on her way.

When I returned to the terrace with my refilled glass,
the sun was perched on the crest of the hills above the
harbor. The sky was orange along the black silhouette, only
to fade into pink and then gradually darken further up. The
town itself was already in semidarkness. It was that un-
certain moment when the day gives in and lets the night
take over. To me, the best time of day.

I lingered, but eventually I couldn't defer it any longer.
It was time to leave.

I tried to take a deep breath in the cooling evening air
as I closed the front door behind me. But my insides seemed

to have contracted, and it felt as if I couldn't fill my lungs properly.

As I came down the stone steps on my way to the harbor, I spotted Pau. Barefoot and wearing shorts, he stood in the doorway of his house, framed by the bright-blue wooden trim. He was smoking and had his eyes on a row of pulled-up stone slabs at his feet. When he heard me, he looked up and smiled.

"*Bona tarda*, Maria. Here I am trying to decide if I should have a go at fixing the drain now or if I should leave it till tomorrow and go upstairs and have my evening drink on the terrace. What do you think?"

"Good evening," I said. I still couldn't make myself try even the simplest phrases in Catalan, not even those I actually knew. "It will soon be completely dark. Perhaps you had better leave it for tomorrow?"

He nodded, stuck the cigarette between his lips, and bent down and lifted one of the slabs and placed it, leaning, against the wall.

"Good advice, thank you. I'll leave it till tomorrow. I'll just move these out of the way for now. Can't have people stumbling on them in the dark." He smiled again, and his teeth shone white in the sudden darkness as the last rays of sun had disappeared behind his house.

"I'm on my way to meet my sister at the bus terminal," I said. I felt as if I had to say something. We usually exchanged a few words when we happened to meet, which was most evenings when I passed his house on the way to have a dinner. It never evolved into a proper conversation. But for some reason, I felt compelled to tell him about Emma's visit. Perhaps I said it more to myself than to him. As if I tried to make Emma's visit into something entirely normal and natural by mentioning it casually, in passing.

"Nice! You will have company for a while. You must be looking forward to that." We waved good-bye, and he continued his work while I carried on down the stairs to the harbor.

I walked slowly, tempted to stop and sit down at one of the cafés. But it was too late, so I carried on toward the bus terminal.

The large new terminal was deserted, and the ticket office looked closed. I sat down on one of the benches but soon stood up again. I just couldn't sit still.

The bus turned into the terminal on time and parked in front of me. The doors opened with a sigh, and the covers to the baggage compartment unfolded like the wings of a giant beetle. There were just a few pieces of luggage inside. A young man jumped off, through the front doors, and picked up a backpack and a bag, leaving only a suitcase.

Then I caught sight of her. She treaded the steps so cautiously, as if hesitant about how to do it. It looked strange. She moved like an old person. Also, her hair was cut very short. I couldn't remember her ever wearing it so short. I felt unpleasantly affected by both observations. When I waved in greeting, she gave me a nod in response. But not even a shadow of a smile. I stepped forward and pulled out what I assumed must be her suitcase.

"Welcome," I said. But when I went to give her a hug, she took a step back, stopping me with a gesture.

"Don't come too close. I was sick for the last part of the trip. I had no idea the road would be so winding. I would have taken a pill had I known."

Now I noticed how pale she was.

I couldn't think of anything to say. Was I expected to apologize for the state of the road?

"It's not far. I hope you'll be okay walking," was what I managed eventually.

"Of course. It'll be nice to get some fresh air. I'll be fine."

I pulled her suitcase behind me, and she made no attempt to take it from me. When we reached the town square, I stopped.

"There, up there, is where the house is," I said, pointing. "Not far at all. But perhaps we should have a bite to eat? Or would you rather go straight home?"

She didn't respond at first, just stood with her eyes on the sea ahead.

"It's so beautiful," she said quietly. "Just as I imagined it."

"Even more beautiful in daylight," I said. "You'll see tomorrow. What do you say? Shall we sit down at one of the places here?" I pointed to the row of small restaurants and bars that lined the square.

She nodded. "Yes, it might be good for me to have something to eat."

We entered a tapas place where I often had my solitary dinners. And I felt a stab of that same stinginess at having to share what I considered mine. As if my enjoyment of the place would somehow be ruined if I shared it with Emma. I had been coming there more or less regularly, and the staff knew me by name, as I knew them. I usually sat at a table in the corner, by the window, and often I brought something to read. They left me undisturbed for as long as I liked. Purposely, I asked for another table when Adriana met us with a smile.

We sat down. And the moment arrived when we had to face each other.

"Thank you for letting me come. I really appreciate it."

"Yes, but I have to admit that I had forgotten the invitation. It was such a long time ago." I realized how this sounded.

She nodded. "Yes, and so much has happened in between. I hope you would have told me if it didn't suit."

"A lot has happened here too, Emma," I said, avoiding her gaze.

"Your partner, is he not here?"

A perfectly natural question. Expected too, and yet it cut straight through my prepared defense. I couldn't even begin to consider a response.

"No, it's just me." It was all I could manage. "Shall we take a look at the menu?"

We placed our orders, and I suppose we managed some kind of stilted conversation, but I have no recollection about what. I was no longer hungry. But as soon as the wine arrived, I took a gulp.

"And Olof? He's not traveling with you?"

Emma lifted her gaze and regarded me with what looked like an almost pleading expression. For a moment, I thought her eyes were brimming with tears, but it could have been the light from the flickering candle on the table. She shook her head.

"No, I've been visiting a friend who has a house near Avignon. That's why I sent you that e-mail. I realized it wasn't far from here. And the train connections are excellent, too."

An obvious evasive maneuver. She was better at it than I was. As she had always been. Already as a child, Emma used to paint beautiful backdrops.

We picked at the food on the plates between us, neither of us with much enthusiasm.

"So you live here permanently now?"

I shrugged. "Not exactly. But I don't live anywhere else either. I suppose you could say that this is the most homelike place I have. I try to take one day at a time. It's peaceful here and I take the odd job every now and then. Jobs I can do from here. I'll see what to do about the future in due course."

"So you're renting? I thought you had bought a house here. It sounded as if you had when you invited me to come and stay."

I stuck some food in my mouth and took my time to chew and swallow.

"I'm thinking about it. But I'm renting for now."

This will be awful, I thought. This mutual prodding into the other's secret hiding places. Not that I was interested in Emma's private life. But I had to say something to avert her questions.

"How are the children?"

She started, as if I had said something unexpected. Then she cleared her throat.

"Fine, just fine, as far as I know."

There was a time when I knew Emma's children. Especially Anna, her oldest. One summer when Anna was nine or ten we spent a couple of weeks together. It was a long time since I had given any thought to those weeks. I had come back to Sweden for a summer holiday, for once. Then, just like now, I had been surprised to hear from Emma. Even more surprised when she asked if I would consider having Anna for a couple of weeks. I never really had an explanation as to why, not at the time, and not later. I knew nothing about Emma's married life. Not what it really was like. After Emma and Olof married, we only saw each other occasionally, at their home. The odd Christmas Eve and birthday, big ones and cause for major celebration. Not mine, certainly not mine. But Mother's, I think. And perhaps Emma's. Her thirtieth, possibly. Mother's sixtieth. I never felt like I belonged at their parties. And I never asked any of them to visit me in London. I didn't feel as if we knew each other at all. Or rather, in a sense I knew Emma, in a way. And Olof. But only as individuals, not as a couple. It was probably my fault. The departing person is responsible for staying in touch. Be that as it may, the fact was that I knew nothing about Emma and Olof together. Not much about them as individuals either, really. Emma insisted on maintaining a facade of us as a happy extended family that celebrated important occasions together. They had a beautiful, generous home, and Emma was an ambitious hostess. As for me, I had to mobilize all the strength I was capable of in order to endure her lavish offerings. And in order to socialize naturally with Olof.

But from the moment I collected Anna that sunny June morning, she and I were the best of friends. It amazed me. I have no children of my own. Children have never really interested me. Not any more than adults do. I don't like children just because they are children, but I like some children because they are interesting human beings. And Anna captured my heart.

She looked like Emma's daughter, absolutely. Beautiful, ethereal, like a little fairy. Blonde and almost translucent. But that was just the surface. Underneath, there was so much that I recognized from myself. Good and bad. So we had our battles during those weeks. And our remarkable high points. Anna learned to dive from the landing. The house I had rented in the archipelago was well equipped, and we had our own little dinghy. So when she had mastered diving from the landing, we rowed to a small islet where there was a high, rounded rock, about six or seven meters high, with deep water below. I watched her knees shake, but then she threw herself into the water without a word. I could feel her apprehension before, as well as her triumph when she had conquered it. I could identify with her, and it felt like a small victory for me too. Evenings, we played chess. As soon as she learned how the pieces moved, she quickly became a strong opponent. She hated losing, and she never gave up. I think I began to love her then.

But over the years that followed, I only saw her sporadically. Until she came to see me in London. She was seventeen then. I hadn't been in touch with her, or with Emma, for a long time, so this meeting was unexpected. But that's what our family is like. Small, sudden bursts of contact, and then silence for years.

I looked up at Emma. I didn't understand what she meant by "as far as I know," but I didn't want to ask. So I let it pass without comment.

"And Olof, how is he?"

For a moment she stared at me, and I thought she looked frightened. Then she looked down and groped for her wineglass. She took several large gulps, drank as if it was water. When she put the glass back, it fell over and wine spilled out over the table.

"Forgive me. I'm so sorry." Emma put her hand over her mouth, and then I was sure there were tears in her eyes. "I'm so clumsy." She was crying audibly.

"Don't worry. It's nothing," I said, and lifted the glass. Adriana came running, carrying a cloth. But before wiping the table, she leaned down over Emma.

"Dip your finger in the wine and touch your forehead." Her English was very good, but Emma stared at her, as if not understanding. "It's bad luck to spill your wine, but if you rub a little of it on your forehead, you turn the bad luck into good luck."

She looked encouragingly at Emma, who hesitantly dipped her finger in the wine and ran it across her forehead.

"There. All is well again," Adriana said, and started to wipe the table. She replaced the tablecloth and made sure all was tidy before she filled Emma's glass. It took only a moment.

But Emma was weeping uncontrollably.

I sat in silence, unsure what to do or say. I gave her the time she needed.

"Olof has left me."

She sat hunched in her chair, and when she again stretched out her hand for the wineglass, it looked as if she was searching for something to hold on to so as not to collapse completely.

I was stunned. Any questions I might have asked seemed

impossible. Any words of comfort, or at least empathy, that I should have been able to produce escaped me. So I lifted my glass and stretched it cautiously across the table.

"We don't need to talk about it now, Emma. We don't need to talk about it at all. You've had a long day. Let's finish the wine and then go back to the house." Emma lifted her glass, and we raised them and let them touch quietly.

I signaled to Adriana that we wanted the bill.

We stepped inside, and I closed the door behind us. Emma stopped and stood with her arms crossed over her chest, embracing herself as if cold. For a moment, standing side by side, it felt as if I was the taller one. This couldn't be right. Emma was five centimeters taller; I knew that for sure. Mother had often pointed it out. I glanced at Emma, but she was looking straight ahead, so I saw her face in profile. She was as beautiful as always, but in some inexplicable way this didn't make the impression on me it had in the past. I wasn't sure I liked the change. There is a kind of reassurance in things remaining the same.

"I thought you could sleep in here." I pointed toward the master bedroom beyond the dining room. "I just have to make the bed. The girl who cleans for me should have been here today, but she never showed up."

I opened the bedroom door and pulled her suitcase

inside. I heard her following behind me as I opened one of the windows.

"You have to make sure the shutters are secured when open, so the wind doesn't catch them. There is no wind right now, but it rises suddenly here."

Emma sank down on the edge of the bed. Again it struck me that she moved so slowly and with such deliberation. Emma who used to tread so lightly. Almost weightless. Now it was as if she could hardly lift her feet. But perhaps she was just tired.

"I'll just pop down and get the bed linen and towels."

So another sudden impulse of mine, I thought, as I walked down the stairs. One with possible consequences. Why had I decided to give her the master bedroom after all? I shook my head. I would probably come to regret this one too.

She helped me make the large double bed, and then I left her to have a shower and unpack. Meanwhile, I put cheese and fruit on a tray and took a bottle of wine from the fridge. Upstairs, on the terrace, I placed the tray on the table and sat down without turning on the lights. The sky slowly filled with stars, more and more the longer I kept my eyes on the black sky. It was as if new layers slowly emerged, as if I dove deeper and deeper into the darkness.

There were no sounds from downstairs. Eventually, I went to see what was taking Emma so long. I knocked on her door and could hear her move inside the room.

"I brought some fruit and cheese upstairs," I said to the

closed door. "Come and join me on the terrace for a little while if you like."

I waited, and finally she opened the door. She wore a sheer white dressing gown and had woolen socks on her feet. She held the top of the gown together, and again I got the impression she was cold.

"I'm not dressed, Maria."

I couldn't help but laugh.

"Doesn't matter here. You can come naked if you like. Nobody will see us up there. We have a stunning view. We're higher up than almost anyone else."

It looked like she tried a little smile.

"Okay, then, for a little while," she said, and followed me up the stairs.

I got us blankets from the lounge, and we wrapped ourselves in them.

"A glass of wine?"

She nodded and I poured. We sat in silence, and the sound of voices occasionally drifted up from the nightlife along the harbor front, as did the constant murmur of the sea. I twirled the glass in my hand. Then I turned to Emma.

"I had in mind to write and let you know that I was very grateful to you for taking care of everything when Mother died," I said. "But somehow I never got around to doing it. So I'm telling you now. I know it was a huge effort. And I don't mean just the funeral. The time before. Most of all that. All of it. All the time."

It surprised me that the words emerged so naturally. She didn't respond.

And that was just as it should be.

I looked up at the stars again and took a deep breath. Perhaps we would get through this after all.

DAY TWO

There was a smell of freshly brewed coffee. I must have sensed it before I woke up. Because for a faint moment I was back in another time. Inside the memory of what it felt like to wake up in the safe knowledge of being loved.

The smell lingered, but the memory quickly dissolved. What remained was just a feeling. An overwhelming sense of regret. I was constantly on alert to keep my memories at bay. It happened less and less frequently that they took me by surprise. The effort of suppressing them had become a natural part of me. I was careful to avoid the triggers. But this one had caught me unawares.

A glance through the window told me that I had slept longer than I had intended. I got out of bed and walked out onto the terrace. It was a little chilly, but the sky was absolutely clear and the white buildings down below shone as if newly washed in the morning sun.

I had made no plans for the day. Not for any day, really. One of the few advantages of my lonely life was that I could allow decisions to evolve naturally. Do what felt right at the moment, and largely avoid making plans for the future. For now anyway. My work did require a measure of discipline. I had the odd deadlines, and I always made sure to meet them. But I had been given the time I needed, largely with no demands, not from the school nor from the gallery in Barcelona. They had allowed me time, and time was really all I had. My time was not freedom, though. It was emptiness. Nothing. But it was what I needed.

I feared that the next few days would affect my existence in some unwanted way. It wasn't just the fact that I didn't know Emma now. I had never really known her. I had no memories of her as a real person of flesh and blood, with a will of her own and a distinct personality. To me, Emma was just a kind of extra in my personal life drama. I realized I knew almost nothing about her. I had no idea what she thought or felt. What she liked. I couldn't remember her ever expressing a firm opinion on anything. Somehow she had only just drifted quietly at the outskirts of my world.

Our childhood had not been conducive to developing hopes or dreams. When I thought about it, I realized that Emma naturally must have had her own thoughts and her own will. She had just been more adaptable, more accepting. We had both struggled to find a way of surviving in the incomprehensible inferno that surrounded us. But separately, rather than together. It felt as if Emma represented something I didn't care to analyze or that required a strength I lacked.

I had no idea what she might hope to get out of this visit. What expectations might she have? Perhaps I ought to plan some excursions. The idea didn't appeal to me, for several reasons. First, I avoided planning my own time, to the extent possible. Second, I certainly didn't want to take responsibility for someone else's pastime. Sure, I often wandered aimlessly in the national reserve. Sometimes for a full day, with my binoculars around my neck and fruit and water in my backpack. I liked the barren landscape that demanded complete focus in order to distinguish colors and details. The shy, darting birds, the plants that from a distance looked so uniform but up close revealed such an extraordinary beauty and spectacular variety. It was an environment that shared its abundance with only the most attentive visitor. I did stroll through the town most days, too, but rarely with a goal or a particular purpose in mind. I often found myself inside the cool, soothing dusk of the cathedral, where time had ceased to exist and where my thoughts were free to roam. My walks were as aimless as everything else in my life.

But now Emma was here, and I wasn't sure what might

be expected of me. I put on my dressing gown and went downstairs.

Emma sat in the small courtyard at the front of the house.

"Do you smoke?" I said, surprised.

She exhaled a thin trail of smoke. "Do you mind? I won't smoke inside, of course."

"Of course I don't mind. I was just a little surprised. I have never seen you smoke before."

"I have made coffee, I hope that was okay, too. It should still be hot."

I went inside to get a cup and returned and sat down opposite Emma.

"I hope I didn't wake you up."

I shook my head. "Absolutely not. I haven't heard a thing. It was the smell of coffee that woke me up."

"Oh, perhaps that was a bad thing?" She looked at me, her head a little cocked.

"No. Not bad at all. Normally, I have to make my own coffee." I took a sip and realized that Emma's coffee was much better than mine.

Only then did I notice the plate with two croissants on the table.

"Have you been out already?"

"Yes, I couldn't sleep so I went for a walk. And I discovered that the bakery was already open."

I tried to ignore it, but it encroached. That creeping,

shameful irritation at my sister invading my private territory. I swallowed a gulp of the strong, bitter coffee.

As she stretched to stub out the cigarette in the tray on the table, I noticed with even greater surprise that her nails were bitten. It was unlike Emma to smoke. But it was inconceivable that she was biting her nails. I raised my gaze, and Emma quickly withdrew her hand and placed it on her lap, out of my sight.

"Have a croissant," she said.

"Thank you, I think I might leave it for a little. I usually have breakfast late. In town. I like sitting there in the morning. With other people around me. And usually time it to coincide with the arrival of the newspapers." I wasn't sure why I felt compelled to tell her this. I was bothered by her presence, but I still invited her into my life in a way I certainly had not intended. It wasn't her fault.

An awkward silence followed and Emma carefully tore off a small piece from one of the croissants. It didn't look as if she was hungry, and instead of putting the piece in her mouth she continued to tear it into ever smaller pieces, while flakes fell through the perforated metal tabletop.

"I usually work between nine and eleven or so, but I'm not very disciplined. I am easily distracted, happy to interrupt my work. And it isn't work, really. I'm on leave from my job at the school in Barcelona. Still, I usually spend a couple of hours in the morning on what I call work. But I am really free to do what I choose with my time. So if there is anything in particular you would like to do, just let me know."

I was grateful that Emma asked no questions. I didn't want to explain, and I didn't want to become entangled in any kind of excuses.

"Oh, don't let me interrupt your routines. I can manage very well on my own. I have no plans at all. I'm happy to do nothing much."

"But surely we should think of something? How about walking to Cap de Creus tomorrow if the weather is good? It's a bit of a walk. Six or seven kilometers but not hard work at all. It should take us an hour and a half, or so, one way. It's beautiful out there, and the lighthouse is famous. We could have lunch at the restaurant. What do you think?"

"I really don't want you to feel that you have to take care of me."

"It's been a while since I was there. I would enjoy it. If you feel like it. Today perhaps you would like to have a look at the town? Let's take a walk a little later. Around eleven or so?"

Emma nodded.

I stood up to go downstairs for my shower, and Emma reached for the packet of cigarettes.

When I returned, she was gone. In her room, I assumed. I filled my coffee cup again and went upstairs to try to get some work done. Or at least make the impression that I had something to do. A justification for still being here. Being alive. If not for others, I needed to do it for me. It was getting gradually harder to silence my conscience. I had been allowed to keep my position at the international school in Barcelona. I realized that they had made an exception, really gone out of their way to support me. But during the time that had passed, I had done nothing much, just the odd temping. A few research reports. So when I sat down at the computer every morning, it wasn't so much to work but to try to maintain some kind of contact with the real world. I did follow the work at the gallery in Barcelona, but I knew that they managed very well without my input. I was officially the owner now, but a very distanced one. At some level I did understand that both the school and the gallery gave me tasks to do for my sake, not theirs. And however awkward it felt initially, I had been forced to admit that it helped. I was well aware that the day when I would have to take the step back was rapidly approaching. It no longer scared me as much as before. Here, in the stillness of this big house, I had been allowed the time I had needed.

There was even less to do than usual. A few e-mails to respond to and a couple of bills to pay, and I was done. So I opened my diary and typed the date.

My sister Emma arrived yesterday. We haven't seen each other since Mother's funeral. I dread the days to come. Can't see how we will get through them. What to do, what to say to each other.

I closed the document and turned off the computer and sat down on the terrace with a book. But I couldn't read either. I had neither heard nor seen Emma, and I didn't plan to go downstairs until it was time for lunch.

Was it like this for other siblings? So impossibly much unsaid between them that every meeting became painful?

I can't remember when I came to understand that we were to have a sibling, Amanda and I. Emma was just there one day. And I can't remember taking much notice of her initially. I had Amanda, and the baby meant nothing to me. But soon I came to realize that Emma changed everything. I have an image of Amanda sitting on the gray sofa with Emma in her arms. She reaches down and whispers something I don't catch. Then she brushes her lips against Emma's forehead. It's just the one picture, but it has never left me.

She helped change the baby, feed her, and pull her around in the stroller. To me, it was as if I had lost a sister. Not gained one. At first I waited impatiently for it to pass. For Amanda to tire of Emma and return to me. But Amanda never tired. She was remarkably steadfast and loyal, even as a small child. Normally, children are so selfish. Or perhaps no more selfish than adults, just unable to hide their true feelings.

But I really don't think that Amanda was ever selfish. This may have affected how I saw myself. How I still see myself. With a sense of inadequacy. Disappointment that I am the person I am. Of course she never abandoned me. But I wanted her whole attention. I wanted everything to be as it had been. I did not want to share Amanda with Emma.

And it didn't pass, either. Quite the opposite. When Emma could walk and began to talk, well, then it got worse, not better. Amanda became the constant babysitter. Wherever we went, she dragged Emma along. In the playground. When we played in the fields behind our house. When we built huts in the forest or played theater. Emma came wherever we went. Amanda's patience and her love had no boundaries. I should have accepted it. Not demanded more than Amanda was able to give. I should have felt secure in the knowledge that she loved me. And I shouldn't have withdrawn. But that is how it is with me. I am unable to share. I would rather go without than be satisfied with crumbs.

The cuckoo clock on the wall in the living room struck eleven, and I stood up. Downstairs, I found Emma where I had left her in the morning, but she had changed and it looked like she had put on a little makeup. When she heard me, she stubbed out her cigarette and stood up.

"Ready?"

Emma nodded and picked up her cardigan from the chair.

᪣

When I arrived in Cadaqués for the very first time, I experienced something I had only heard described: an immediate sense of belonging. As if I instinctively knew the place inside and out without having to explore it. It has been many years since that first time. Then, much later, when Maya and I arrived here together, and I tried to explain to her how I felt, she just put her hand on my arm, looked at me, and said with a light laugh: "I know, Maria. I feel exactly the same."

But here I was, strolling with my sister Emma. It was impossible for me to know what she was thinking. And difficult to acknowledge that I didn't really want to know. We walked slowly along the quay. Some of the little boats were already pulled out of the sea, and several of the touristy shops had closed for the season.

Ever since I was a child, I have loved the autumn. There is a melancholy seriousness about it that has always appealed to me. It is as if everything becomes clearer and sharper, and a liberating stillness descends after the intense activities of the summer.

"I can understand why you like it here, Maria."

"You do?" I said, laughing a little. "You have hardly seen anything yet. And we hardly know each other after all these years. If we ever did."

"I can still feel that this place fits you. Or that you fit this place."

We walked to the square, and I bought my newspaper. I wouldn't be able to read it at the café as usual, so I folded it and stuck it in my basket.

"You were right, Maria."

I glanced at Emma, wondering what she meant.

"It's even more beautiful in daylight." She looked out over the sea. "I actually imagined it to be like this. Every time I thought of you, I saw you in a place like this. And always by the sea."

"Oh, that surprises me a little, Emma. First, I'm surprised that you have thought about me at all. And, second, that you have placed me by the sea, because I have never imagined myself by the sea, any sea. I can really only remember one holiday by the sea, and that was the year when I rented a cottage in the archipelago and Anna came and stayed with me for a couple of weeks."

"Yes, it is strange. I realize that when I think about it. But when I saw how happy you looked when we stood there after Mother's funeral, I had a vision of you living someplace like this. By the sea. In the sun."

I wasn't sure what to say, and to gain a little time I searched my basket for my sunglasses. It felt like a relief to put them on.

"Shall we go and sit down at the café over there?" I asked, finally. We sat down and ordered coffee and toast, and Emma lit a cigarette.

"Do you swim in the sea?"

I shook my head.

"Me neither."

Suddenly neither of us seemed to find anything to say, and the silence sat between us, heavy and immobile.

"Would you like to see some pictures of Anna and Jakob?" Emma said eventually.

I nodded, grateful for the interruption, and Emma pulled out her phone and clicked to show pictures of her children. She placed the phone on the table and opened one picture at a time. I recognized them, of course. I had seen them at the funeral two years before. But there were some recent close-ups of Anna I hadn't seen. And I was unprepared for how she had changed. There were only a few pictures, and they all seemed to have been taken at the same occasion. She wore a gray hooded jersey and her hair was very short. But what affected me was to see how very thin she was. That and her eyes. In my mind I had kept an image of the ten-year-old Anna, so excited to try anything new she could barely contain herself. But the Anna that lay between us on the table looked straight at us, with no expression at all. This was the one picture where she really looked into the camera. In all the others it seemed as if she had rather not wanted to be photographed or had perhaps not been aware of it.

I have never really known Emma's Jakob. When he was a child, I saw him only as an attachment to Emma. She was very protective of him. I remember thinking that she treated the children very differently, although they'd been born only two years apart. This might have contributed to my feelings for Anna. But here I could see the young man that Jakob had become. I could see that he resembled Emma, more so than Anna did now that they were adults. But Jakob had Olof's brown eyes.

"Nice pictures," I said. "So good to get to see them. I saw them at the funeral, of course. And Anna came to see me in London a few years ago. But apart from that, I'm not sure how many years it's been since I saw either of them. To me, it's as if they've gone from young children to adults with no childhood in between."

Emma looked at me, her brows furrowed.

"There may be something to that," she said.

I couldn't quite interpret her expression, so I made no comment.

"After Anna left home, we only saw her sporadically and often there were long gaps between her visits. She would appear without a warning, only to disappear for months without being in touch. In a way, I was surprised when she turned up at the funeral. I had hoped she would come, of course. But she didn't like Mother. So perhaps she wanted to see it with her own eyes. See that Mother did not exist anymore." Emma gave a joyless laugh.

"Yes, I think I might have felt something similar. People

have such diverse and sometimes strange reasons for attending funerals. I think I may have been hoping for some kind of closure."

I stopped, surprised at my words. I hadn't really known this was how I felt about Mother's funeral.

"That's why I came, I think. But it didn't really help. I don't know why I thought it would. You are forever attached to your mother. There had been so many years since we last met, Mother and I. At your place, probably. It might have been one of those Christmases we had together. And, as usual, I felt invisible. It was as if she had no interest in my life at all. I realize now that she had ended our relationship long before. She had no daughter, but I still had a mother. And I was reminded of how it felt to be completely ignored by someone who should be central in your life. In spite of everything, I suppose in a twisted way Mother always was. And however much I fought my feelings, they welled up. As they do now, when we talk about it." I struggled to hold back tears and swallowed repeatedly.

"You are mistaken, Maria. Completely mistaken."

I didn't want to hear what she had to say, and I signaled the waiter. He approached, and I paid the bill, in spite of Emma's protests.

"It will balance out. You can pay for dinner one evening. Shall we walk to the cathedral?"

Emma nodded and we left.

I am not religious. Not surprising perhaps. I can't remember that we ever went to church when I was growing up or that anybody ever talked about religion. I was baptized, though. Amanda and I were, probably because it was touch and go whether we were going to survive when we were born. But I was not confirmed. And if I had ever married, it would not have been in a church. But this rather modest church, which is yet referred to as "The Cathedral" by the locals, and which looks as if it watches the whole town where it sits perched on a high hill, is special to me. A kind of peace fills me when I enter. Often I am the only person inside, and nothing disturbs me. I can simultaneously enter my innermost self and abandon myself entirely. It is difficult to describe. I have not experienced anything like it anywhere else.

So it was with a measure of trepidation that I wandered up the narrow streets with Emma. I was going to share with her another place that I would have liked to keep to myself. But she would not understand my feelings. To her, I was just taking her on a little tour of the town, including the church.

We stepped inside the cool darkness. It is not a particularly ornate church, and I doubt that there is anything culturally or historically exceptional about it, even though the baroque altarpiece is almost obscenely extravagant. But Emma wanted to wander around and see what there was to see. I sat down at the end of one of the front pews. The whole space lay in half darkness, but I could see a few candles flickering inside some of the small side chapels, and there was a faint smell of wax in the air. I closed my eyes.

When I looked up again, a while later, I realized I was alone. Emma must have slipped out without my noticing.

She stood, leaning against the white wall, in the blinding sunlight outside. She had her face half-turned away from me, looking out over the sea below. And I saw her for the first time as she would appear to someone who didn't know her. We carried such a long past, the two of us. We had somehow been given parts in the same play, without really understanding what it was about. We had played along, year after year, together yet not together at all. Whether we wanted it or not, we were inevitably connected by our common past. And they blocked the view, all those years. But in that brief moment when I spotted her there, outlined against the intensely blue sea, I thought I could see what my sister actually looked like.

I realized that Emma was no longer young. Here was a decidedly middle-aged woman. Nor was she as beautiful as I had always thought. It was as if something had left her forever. Not just her youth, but a part of her personality. Something that used to hold her up, had given her that proud bearing and the natural elegance.

And the realization made me want to weep.

I didn't want to see what life had done to Emma. On no

condition did I want to be pulled into her life. Become aware of her needs. I really had no wish to have anything to do with her at all. Before she appeared here in Cadaqués I had thought Mother's death had cut the last tie between us.

But here I was, struggling to control my feelings.

She must have become aware of my presence, and she turned and waved. I slowly wandered over and joined her by the wall.

"I don't like churches," she said. "So I had to get out. Those dark spaces make me feel utterly forlorn. I wandered around and looked at the artwork, the paintings and sculptures. Not one image of a happy person. Just grief, pain, and sorrow. People killing each other, torturing each other. But not one single happy human being. Not one smile. I just can't cope."

It was so unexpected that I couldn't think of anything to say. What she said was as wrong as her bitten nails and the cigarettes. I just couldn't reconcile it with the Emma I remembered. The Emma who had always wanted to smooth over even the slightest unpleasantness. Make everything pretty.

"Oh, I just sit down inside and allow the stillness to take over," I said eventually. "It feels like I can put myself aside for a moment. Be released from having to carry everything that is me. At the same time, I feel as if I am able to reconnect to something fundamental."

I laughed, a little embarrassed. Why did I tell her this?

"I'm not sure how to explain it. It has nothing to do with religion. But it has helped me."

Emma's blue eyes regarded me for a moment. "I envy you that, Maria."

⚜

We did our grocery shopping on the way back and arrived home for a late lunch. Emma offered to make a salad, and I accepted gratefully and went upstairs and sat down by the computer.

I opened my diary again.

She asks for nothing. She is awfully easy to deal with. And yet she completely overwhelms me with her very presence. She already interferes with everything I do, just by being here. I wish that I had never heard from her. Or that I had never issued that damned invitation. Because now it would make no difference even if she left today. It is already too late.

I sat staring at my own words. I could hear Emma working in the kitchen below. My sister was making lunch for us. I should be happy having her here. Normal sisters would laugh and chat and be comfortable together. But we moved as if walking on thin ice, scared that it might crack under our feet at the first misstep. Was that just me? Or was it equally awkward for Emma?

I closed the computer and went downstairs to help with lunch.

When we had eaten, we sat together on the terrace, Emma with her slim white legs in the sun and her upper body in the shade. I sat completely in the shade.

"How do you pass the time when you are by yourself here?"

"Time passes regardless, doesn't it?"

"Ah, you know what I mean. What do you do when you're not working? Doesn't it get lonely and . . . well, empty?"

I struggled to defend my aimless existence even to myself. I was ashamed of my empty life. So much harder, then, to justify it to Emma. Suddenly I felt a wave of unreasonable rage well up inside. What right did she have to question my life?

"What about you? How do you fill your days?" I said instead. "I don't even know if you have a job."

Emma was reclining in the sun chair and had closed her eyes, as if blinded by the sun that didn't even reach her face. Her response took a moment. Finally, she turned her head and looked at me.

"You, you have always had a job. Gone from one good position to another as it has pleased you, never having to worry."

"Strange description of my life. But, sure, I have always worked. I have supported myself since I left school. So, yes, that's correct. If I have worried, you know nothing about it. And it's none of your business."

Emma nodded slowly.

"Fair enough. I'm sorry. I didn't mean to pry. But to answer your question, no, I don't have a job. It's been a long time. First I stayed at home with the children. And then it wasn't that easy to find something. Mariefred is such a small place. We moved there because that's where Olof's job was. It was a good place for the children too . . . So, well, that's where we ended up."

I waited for her to continue.

"Unlike you, I have no real education. Father thought it was ridiculous when I wanted to go to art school."

"But, God, you were an adult by then! Surely you could have decided for yourself?"

Emma shrugged. "That's not how it felt at the time. So I did a one-year course. Business Administration, it was called. But we really learned how to become secretaries, unaware that we trained for jobs that would soon disappear. It didn't matter much, though. I only worked a few years before we married. But you know all this."

The conversation was drifting in an uncomfortable direction. I didn't want to talk about Emma's life. Certainly not about her father. And not about her and Olof. So I gave her what she asked for. An outline of my lonely life.

"Like I said before, I do a little work in the morning. Then I take a few hours off. On good days I work in the afternoon too. And sometimes in the evening. But I am my own master, so sometimes I take a day off and go for a hike in the hills with my binoculars. There is rich and interesting birdlife here."

"That sounds like a very free life."

"It is. For now. I am working on a thesis in historical linguistics. But it's something I have been working on for several years. I may never complete it."

What I had just said surprised me. I had given no thought to my abandoned thesis for a long time. To my great relief, she asked nothing further.

"You don't have a car?"

"Haven't felt the need for one. I'll see. If I decide to stay, I may get one."

This line of questioning felt even more awkward. Where were her questions leading?

"It's not always easy to remember, in hindsight, what you once hoped for or had in mind. And, you know, Emma, it's hardest when all your circumstances have altered, none of it your own doing. When nothing at all is as it was when you once made your decision."

Emma was lying with her eyes closed again. I wasn't sure if she was listening. But then she spoke again.

"Just recently, it struck me that I have not made a single decision. Small things, yes. Unimportant little decisions, sure. But none of the large, life-changing ones. It is as if I have just drifted along aimlessly all my life. I realized that I haven't even allowed myself to feel very much. Perhaps because it would be too painful to admit that my life was the result of other people's decisions. As if I had never really existed."

She sat up in the chair, with her legs pulled up and her arms around them. She looked out over the sea.

"But then I realized it actually is a decision, this *not* making any decisions. It is deciding to shirk, to give the responsibility to someone else."

She turned her head and looked at me.

"But I don't know how to do it. Even the smallest decision fills me with apprehension. You have no idea how hard it was to write that e-mail to you."

I searched desperately for something to say.

"It's probably impossible for you to understand, Maria."

She didn't sigh, but as she returned her gaze to the sea, it was as if her whole body gave a long sigh.

I stood up and leaned on the railing. The metal was still warm under my hands. I still couldn't think of a proper response and felt increasingly self-conscious.

"Do you ever think about Mother?"

The question appeared out of the blue. I had no idea what had prompted me to ask it.

"Of course I do. Don't you?"

I shook my head. "No, I have tried to teach myself not to."

"Easy for you, perhaps. You were not there."

"Well, seventeen years is a long time. I was there all those years. My whole childhood, my youth."

"Were you? Were you really there, Maria? Were you ever present in any of our lives? I remember how I longed for you when you had left. How I missed your presence, even though you never seemed to notice me. It would have helped just knowing that you were asleep in the room next to mine. When you disappeared, it was as if the light dimmed. It became harder to see. And I could find no way out. Do you know, Maria, that was when I became a prisoner? That was when I lost the strength, the hope of ever getting away."

I heard her rise from the chair. She took the cigarette pack from her pocket and looked at me for permission. I nodded, and she lit one and inhaled deeply. I thought I could see how it calmed her. Or comforted her. We stood there, side by side, leaning against the railing.

"Of course, it was not your fault. Nothing seems to be anybody's fault when you look back. It's as if everything just aimlessly happened. Evolved without anybody's interference, and turned into a hopeless mess. A chaos where all you could do was to sit on the edge, hold on for your life, and hope that eventually a pattern would emerge. That something would point you in some direction. That somehow you would survive. Or at least that it would pass. That there would be an end."

She exhaled. A white, sheer cloud of smoke left her lips and lifted. I couldn't take my eyes off her. The cropped blonde hair. The classical profile against the afternoon sky. And that cloud of smoke. For a second, I wished I had my camera available. And then I was ashamed that I had even had the thought.

She stubbed out the cigarette and began to gather the plates and glasses from the table.

"Just take what you can manage. I'll take the rest," I said. She nodded but said nothing. Then she turned and walked a little unsteadily across the floor toward the glass doors.

For a moment, I was overcome by an impulse to stretch out my hand. To ask her to stay a little while. Talk to me a little longer.

"Think about that walk tomorrow. You don't need to decide now."

It looked like she stopped in her tracks. Then she turned to face me.

"All of this is yours, Maria. Isn't it? You found it. You chose it. You pay for it. Even if you don't own it, it is yours."

The sound of a scooter passing in the alleyway below silenced her for a moment.

"You know what, Maria? I have never had anything

that was mine. Nothing. I wonder if you can understand what it is like to have nothing."

She carried on and disappeared down the stairs.

During the past year, I had learned to just let time pass. Allow hours and days to pass, often unable to tell what day or week it was. It was easier for me to tell the time of day. A quick glance out over the sea below was all I needed.

I don't know what I did after lunch. I sat in front of my laptop. Listened to music. Wrote a few lines in my strange diary. Responded to some e-mails. And when I looked up, it was late afternoon. I thought I had heard Emma leave the house at some stage, but I had not heard her return. So I was startled when I heard her voice from downstairs. Hers and a man's. I stood up and looked out the window over-looking the entrance below, but I couldn't see anybody. Then I heard the front door open and now the voices came from the kitchen.

When Emma called my name, I suddenly felt stupid. As if I was hiding. I walked quickly down the stairs.

Pau and Emma stood by the kitchen counter, and it looked like Emma was making coffee.

"I came by to ask if you would like to come for a trip in my boat," Pau said, and gave me quick peck on the cheek. "It will soon be time to take it out of the water, and I thought it might be fun for Emma to see a little more of the coast."

I glanced at Emma but couldn't quite read her expression. It felt awkward to stand there, with Pau in my kitchen again. For the first time in such a long time. And I didn't like that it had been Emma who let him in.

"What do you say, Emma?" I could hear that I sounded curt, but I couldn't think of anything to add.

It felt like she took a little too long to respond.

"Oh, I'm not sure. I don't want you to feel like you have to look after me. I am happy just to stroll around . . ."

"It's no bother at all. The boat and I both need a last outing. You choose a day that suits. We can bring lunch and anchor in a bay somewhere. The weather is supposed to hold until after the weekend, I think."

We looked at each other, Emma and I. I wondered what she was thinking. If, like me, she weighed the advantage of having a third person around, to avoid being pulled into painful personal conversations, against the effort of pretending to be two normal sisters for a whole day.

"That sounds absolutely lovely," she said finally. She gave Pau a warm smile and suddenly she was my beautiful sister again.

"It's decided, then! How about Monday?"

We nodded. And we smiled. But our thoughts we kept to ourselves.

❧

It was a glorious evening with a warm sunset. We decided to take a walk and then have dinner at one of the restaurants in the harbor. It was Friday, so more people were about. Local tourists from Barcelona and Girona who had arrived for the weekend. We walked along the quay and carried on toward Punta des Bou Marí. We walked slowly. After the nice day, people lingered on the beach. A couple was floating closely together, farther out. Two dark heads close together on the mottled surface.

"I can't let it go, what you said earlier. That you never think of Mother," Emma said suddenly.

"Why? I mean, why should I be thinking of her?"

"Because she used to think of you, perhaps? I was always compared with you."

I snorted. "That must be your imagination, Emma."

She stopped abruptly.

"All my life people have said things like that to me, Maria. I don't want you to do that. I have not imagined this. I know it. Unlike you, I was there. I have lived my whole life close to Mother. And I was there when she realized she was going to die. I know that she was thinking of you."

I slowed down, but I still carried on without looking back.

"But you may not know what she was thinking?" I said over my shoulder. "What people say they are thinking and what they are actually thinking are often very different matters. Also, we are not able to control our thoughts, even though I wish I could. So you tell me that you know Mother was thinking of me, but neither you nor I know what she was thinking. Nor is it necessarily a given that it is positive to be thinking about another person."

Emma didn't answer, but she had caught up with me.

"Do you really have no positive memories of Mother?"

I said nothing.

"Not even early ones? When you were little, Amanda and you?"

I stopped in my tracks and looked at her.

"No, I'm telling you! I keep those memories away from me, because they are painful. Mostly, I remember absence. My hopeless longing for intimacy. For love. Or even a small measure of interest. But Mother lived in a world where there was only room for her. We were just props. Of interest only for as long as she needed us. I'm not sure, we might have filled some purpose initially, Amanda and I. I have seen pictures of us when we were little. Prettily dressed and styled, as if on display. To be admired perhaps. Like dolls or ornaments. Even Father might have been no more than an accessory. Or at least his infinite, unrequited love was. We might have managed to give the impression of a happy family for some time. If so, I have no memories of it.

And as you know, Mother's interest was always fleeting. When you were born, her focus seemed renewed. Everything looked beautiful. There was money then too. But I think I understood how quickly her interest faded. How the arguments started again. And how soon your father began to look at me. Come sit on my bedside to say good night. His disgusting tears and prayers for a little comfort in his loneliness. His wet kisses. It was revolting."

I was gasping for air. This was precisely what I had dreaded. And had been determined to avoid at all costs.

"Before you arrived, we managed, Amanda and I. We were lonely, but we had each other. And we had Father. And for a few years, we had Grandfather. We had summer holidays at his house in Dalarna. There were bright moments. But then darkness descended."

"To me, it always seemed bright when I was with Amanda and you."

"Now when I think about that time—something I hope I will never have to do again—I can see things I didn't see then. I can see that you were little and innocent. And I can see that it was as hard for you as it was for Amanda and me. Worse, I think. Lonelier even. I can see that. But it changes nothing. I can't change how I feel."

I felt unable to stop. What gushed out of me seemed like a long speech in my defense. But Emma gave me no response. No comments, no questions. No reaction at all. So I continued.

"It was as if Mother could never see beyond herself. All of us, we were only there for her sake. And only for as long as she had need of us. It was always about her. Her needs. And her needs were always something other than what she had. She went from one place to another. From one man to another. And along her path we lay strewn, all of us that she no longer needed. You and me. And your father as well as mine. And all the other discarded men. We lay there, all of us. All the love she was unable or unwilling to embrace. I don't think her restless search ended until she died."

We walked in silence for a little while.

"As long as I had Amanda, I managed anyway. What we had was forever. Nothing could threaten our love. Later . . . Well, later I came to realize that absolutely nothing is forever."

Emma stopped and placed her hand on my arm.

"You said we often don't know what we think, Maria. Perhaps we are even less aware of our emotions. What influences them. You and I, we can both recall our mother. But what we see is only the surface. From our own respective perspectives. Perhaps we are just as selfish as she was? So preoccupied by our own unsatisfied needs that we are unable to see her as a human being? Neither of us knows her innermost thoughts and feelings. Her dreams and hopes. And, like you said, she might not have understood them herself. Or been able to control them."

Emma's voice was so soft I took a step closer to hear her properly.

"Mother might have been as unhappy as we were."

I stopped.

"But we were her children, Emma. We needed her. Instead, she seemed to view us as something there to satisfy her needs. Briefly. Until she resumed her search for something else."

To my horror, I realized I had started to weep. It took all my strength to try to suppress the sobs that threatened to escape from my chest.

Emma's hand stroked my arm lightly.

"Let's turn back," she said.

We walked back the same way, not talking much. I soon noticed that Emma seemed to struggle to keep up and slowed my pace again. Since I didn't get much other exercise, I had made a point of walking briskly when I was out. I had nobody else to consider, so my pace was entirely my own. I thought it a bit strange that it felt as if Emma needed to walk more slowly, but since she said nothing about it, I asked nothing.

It wasn't until we had eaten and ordered coffee that our conversation turned to Mother again. Emma took an envelope from her handbag and placed it on the table.

"You made it very clear that you wanted nothing from Mother's estate. I only took a few small items myself.

Neither Anna nor Jakob wanted anything. What remained, I sold or disposed of. It wasn't worth very much. But this I brought for you."

She passed the envelope across.

"But I told you I wanted nothing."

"Do with it what you want. Throw it away unopened if you wish."

"It would have been better if you had never made me aware of it."

"I brought it because I think you should have it. You may not feel like it now. But you may change your mind. Anyway, I though you should have it."

Reluctantly I picked up the envelope and stuck it quickly into my handbag.

Back home, we walked upstairs to the terrace. It was another clear, starry night, and I didn't turn on the light. We sat in the deck chairs with blankets over our laps.

"It would have been easier if Olof had left me for another woman," Emma said suddenly. "If he had met someone, I mean. Someone he desired. As it is, he just didn't want me. There is nothing positive in it for either of us."

There was a pause and the sound of the sea filled the air, like a constant, soothing breathing.

"And you? Did you want to continue?" I wasn't sure what made me ask.

"I have loved Olof since the first time I saw him, when you brought him home that autumn before Amanda died."

"But you were just a little kid then." I could hear how skeptical, almost scornful, I sounded.

"Children can love as well as adults. Perhaps more. Deeper and stronger. And more lasting. That's how it was for me anyway."

She tucked the blanket closer until her body was completely covered.

"It was a miracle."

I threw her a questioning glance.

"At first it was a tragedy, of course. A tragedy in stages. First Amanda's death. The overriding, unfathomable tragedy. Then you disappeared with Olof. It was like you gradually moved to his family. Initially you were gone a few days. Then weeks. Until I realized that you no longer lived with us. But, then, at least I got to see you occasionally, you and Olof. I knew you were still in town. It was different from knowing you slept in the room next to mine, but it was something. You were there. I could bump into you. The very last bit of hope disappeared when you left Olof and went away. I knew then that I had lost all those I loved. Amanda. You. And Olof. I had no idea how I would survive. It was as if you had taken everything with you. My world became so very silent. The only sound was the arguments. It was as if I had never really heard them before. But now they filled the entire apartment, and I had no means to shut them out."

"I heard them all the time. And they were always followed by those visits to my room."

"But you had me, Maria. I saw you. Even if it meant nothing to you, I was there."

And I did remember how she had often stood beside my bed. Quiet and serious in her crumpled nightgown and with her one-legged teddy bear in her hand. I remembered that I never allowed her to crawl into my bed. How instead I turned to the wall until I could hear her return to her room. I knew now that it was cruel. Because I always knew what she longed for. And I never gave it to her.

I didn't want to remember that.

"So it was a miracle when Olof returned to my life. Such a long time had passed. Several years. He had done his military service and was at university in Uppsala. While I hadn't been doing much at all. That's what it felt like. But one day he was back, and it was as if he held open the door to real life. And finally I could come inside. Or outside, rather. I could step out into life. Not exactly participating but surrounded by it, at least. I was happy just to be allowed to exist there."

I thought about what it had been like for me. Olof had certainly not represented real life to me. Rather the opposite. He had blocked the path to the life I so desperately wanted. His love and his expectations blocked everything. And it became worse when I moved in with him and his family. I remembered his understanding, kind parents. His welcoming brothers. Everything that surrounded me there was filled with warmth. And I remembered how it began to suffocate me.

"At first, all I hoped was that he would continue to stay near me. That I would be allowed to see him. Listen to him talk. I don't think I ever imagined that he would fall in love with me. Because he was still yours, Maria. Even if we hardly ever talked about you, you were there, between us. At least for me. I can see now that I never stopped feeling that. Olof never really became mine. That's a ridiculous expression, by the way. No person ever belongs to anybody else. But I think you get what I mean. I just wasn't able to believe that he loved me. Perhaps that's why his love eroded until there was nothing left? Because I never believed in it?"

It sounded as if she was genuinely searching for an answer to her own question, but I had nothing to say. The Olof I had once known had nothing in common with the man I later met as Emma's husband and the father of her children. I was no longer certain what I felt for him. If I had felt anything at all, other than an instinctive need to flee my own home. A search for a safe haven. Maybe that was all it had ever been. And maybe that was why it became intolerable when I realized what was expected of me.

"I don't think we are responsible for the love that is offered to us. Grateful, possibly. But not responsible. Love is not fair. You don't get in proportion to what you give. And you can never make someone love you."

"True. But you may still need to learn to appreciate what is given to you. Not just discard it as insufficient. It may be all the love you will get. Perhaps now I'm just scared of living my own life. It may not be grief I feel, but selfish dread."

I could hear that she was crying.

"It is scary to realize that you are alone. But you may rightly question how much of an illusion the security of a relationship really is. Everything can be taken from us at any time. We have to manage to be alone."

"I'm afraid of so many things, Maria. Not just for my own sake. I'm afraid of how my children will fare. Anna lives alone in London. I can see that she is doing well professionally. She is a graphic designer with a firm there and you can see her work online. But she has had an eating disorder since she was fourteen. You saw what she looked like at the funeral. It is worse now. It's been up-and-down through the years. Mostly down lately. She never talks about it, and I can't ask. Jakob is studying economics in Stockholm. He is doing well, but he seems very lonely. He has always had trouble finding friends, and he fared badly at school. Sometimes I wonder if I have shaped them, if I've been a bad role model when it comes to relationships."

"I don't know anything about children. Not much about relationships either. I have no idea how much of an influence parents have. I would like to think that it is not that determining. That we continue to grow as adults and can fill in what is missing from our childhood. But I don't know. In my best moments, I like to believe that it can be done. That I can choose how I regard myself. How I regard my existence and how I regard the world around me. I feel like I have fought against being limited by my background ever since I was a small child. I didn't want to become like Mother. I realized that I didn't want to become a mother either. I never felt confident that I would be up to that enormous task."

Emma stood up. Softly she placed her hand on my head. It was a gentle caress, her hand hardly touched. Yet it affected me with unexpected force.

"Perhaps we are more alike than either of us ever believed," she said. "Good night, Maria. Dream something beautiful."

With that she disappeared inside.

DAY THREE

I dreamed about Amanda. But even though I remained absolutely still, with my eyes closed, and tried to hold on to the dream, it faded inexorably. She had been holding me, and I had felt her warm breath on my cheek. But what she had whispered in my ear was lost. I rarely thought about her consciously nowadays. But she was a constant presence, just like my own body. She was part of me. It still happened that I was overwhelmed by grief at the fact that she no longer existed. I could be struck by a longing to hear her voice, smell her scent. To be surprised by her thoughts and ideas. But everything that was Amanda inside me now was just a product of my memories and what I had added later.

It was early, and the sun was still just a hint in the east. I wrapped the blanket around me and sank down into one of the deck chairs. Dew covered everything, and the town below was completely still and silent.

I felt left out here too. As is if the place withdrew and no longer included me. Or else it was I who was unable to embrace the place completely. Perhaps I am afraid to abandon myself, not just in relation to other people, but also to places. I can't remember feeling fully at home any-where. Sometimes when I read or hear about people's rela-tionships to places I feel sad that I don't have such a place or such a relationship.

I was hopeful when we found the house and began to envisage what it would be like to move here. Now I will never know if I would have settled in if all had gone ac-cording to plan. As it is, I have to make do with the sense of peace that I can still experience here.

I thought about Amanda. She was sixteen years old the last time I saw her. But because I carry her with me all the time, I imagine she would have developed more or less like me. A bizarre assumption, really. I do want to think that we were two sides of one and the same individual. But this is not true, of course. Amanda was not like me. Superfi-cially we did look alike. Identical twins are confusingly similar. We would probably have looked more or less alike now too. But Amanda's life would not have evolved like mine. And mine would probably not have looked like it does. It is impossible to imagine things that never happened.

I stood up and went downstairs to the kitchen. I realized that I expected Emma to be up before me again, but there were no signs of her, so I assumed she was still asleep. I made coffee and opened the front door. When I am by myself, I seldom use the small patio, but for some reason I now sat down at the round table with my coffee. It surprised me to realize that I was looking forward to Emma's appearance.

But she took her time, and eventually I went downstairs to have a shower and dress. The sun had risen when I returned to the kitchen, and it looked like it was going to be another fine day. I considered going down to buy bread, but before I had made a decision, I heard Emma open the bedroom door. She looked tired, as if she had had a sleepless night.

"Good morning," she said, and walked slowly toward me. She was barefoot and wearing her white dressing gown. It hung loosely on her thin frame, and her short blonde hair lay smooth over her head. Suddenly I had a vision of a hospital patient. I poured a cup of coffee and held it out to her. She took it and slowly walked outside. I took my cup and followed.

"It looks like another fine day," I said, just to say something. Emma didn't respond.

"What do you say? Do you feel like a walk to Port Lligat? We could visit Salvador Dalí's home. I have seen it before, of course, but each time I return I discover something new. I can call and find out if there is room on a guided tour."

Emma had lit a cigarette. She looked at me with a pensive expression.

"No need to do anything much at all for my sake, Maria. As you can see, I am not in great shape."

"But it's just a short walk. Fifteen minutes or so. Just up the hill behind us and down into the next bay. You walk along the road, and we can take our time. I think you'll enjoy it."

It took a moment before she answered.

"I have been ill," she said eventually. "I can't manage as much as I used to. At least not for now."

"I'm sorry. I had no idea." I gave her an inquiring look. "Do you want to talk about it?"

She shook her head.

"Of course you didn't know. I am much better now. And I'll get better still. I'm just tired, that's all. But I'd rather not talk about it. I just thought I should explain why I'm so slow. A short walk today will be just fine. You don't have to walk at my slow pace, though."

Ever since she stepped off the bus, I had been surprised at how changed she appeared. Now I was relieved that she had volunteered a kind of explanation. Even if she hadn't said much. I felt I couldn't really ask anything further. It had to be on her terms.

"Of course we'll walk together."

When we had climbed the steep slope and reached the top, we stopped to enter the small chapel. The entrance to the cemetery was open, but Emma shook her head.

"No thanks. Not for me. But I'm happy to follow you into the chapel."

I'm not sure why, but I have become more and more fascinated by religious buildings of various kinds. Perhaps I am searching for something inside them. This particular small whitewashed chapel had especially touched me ever since I first saw it. Perhaps more than the cathedral in town. The chapel doesn't seem to be used for regular services, but it always looks clean and well kept. As if someone is looking after it. The white walls are largely lacking decorations. The whole space is simple and unadorned. We sat down on one of the wooden benches.

"It's brighter here," said Emma. "Here, even I might find a little peace."

Unexpectedly, it was as if we both managed to find a moment of rest. We remained in the cool, light room for quite a while.

On our way downhill we stopped now and then to take in the view. It was difficult to understand that it was October. Little white sailing boats drifted on the sparkling sea in the distance and the olive trees' gray-green foliage shaded the slope below us. Emma stood with her hands resting on the top of the wall that ran along the road.

"I can understand why he wanted to live here."

"Who?"

"Salvador Dalí, of course. That's his house down there, isn't it?"

She pointed toward the white house down by the sea. It wasn't one house, really, but a collection of small buildings that had been connected. I had often compared it to Carl Larsson's house in Sundborn. A home that had been allowed to grow organically as needs had required and ideas had been realized. The result of different kinds of investments: creative, practical, and financial. And an expression of the owner's personality. As different from my own home as one could imagine. My house was no expression of my personality at all. It was a protection. A fortress.

We had a knowledgeable and pleasant young guide, and the group of visitors seemed genuinely interested in what she had to tell. As for me, I struggled to muster much interest this time. The rooms seemed somehow more faded and dustier than during my previous visits. It saddened me. When we had wandered through the public parts of the buildings, we were left to explore the garden on our own. Emma and I walked up to the top of the hill and inside the small building that sat on its own up on the highest point. Inside, a black-and-white documentary was playing on a loop, and there were chairs placed along the wall. We sat down. The film contained short clips from Dalí's life as well as interviews with him. It struck me that his ever-present wife never seemed to have a word to say. Yet she was such a strong presence in their home. And in Dalí's art. But perhaps this was as it should be. Perhaps a muse has to maintain a measure of mystique behind her secretive smile. And who knows what their relationship might have been when they were alone, without an audience?

After the semidarkness inside, we were blinded by the sun as we came outside. Emma put on her sunglasses.

"Did you hear what he said? About his dead brother? A brother he had never met but whose name he was given. During his entire childhood, he felt his parents were really addressing his brother when they used his name. That they continued to love the lost child through the living. And he later realized he was forced to kill the brother inside in order to be able to live his own life."

Emma seemed to be deeply touched.

"I don't know why, but it struck me that perhaps I became Mother's only child. That I was all three of us. And at the same time never really felt as if I existed." She looked at me with an awkward smile.

"I'm talking nonsense. I was just so strangely affected by that part about the brother. But I think it's time for something to eat now."

"Yes, it's lunchtime, absolutely. There is a small place a little further on. Simple, but their grilled fish is nice."

We walked slowly along the beach, and suddenly I felt Emma stick her hand under my arm. I wasn't sure if it was because she needed support or for some other reason. But, either way, I allowed it to happen.

We had grilled prawns, cuttlefish, and halibut and drank the local white wine.

"It feels a little odd to sit here and have wine in the middle of the day." Emma lifted her glass and toasted. "A little wicked. And wonderful."

The friendly owner walked between the tables and chatted to the guests. He recognized me and gave me a wide smile as he approached. Maya and I had often eaten here. But it felt like a long time ago.

"I brought my sister today," I said, and introduced them to each other. "Emma has come to stay with me for a few days."

Marcello turned to Emma and asked a few polite questions. Emma smiled and suddenly she seemed to relax. It was as if she had a social persona that she was able to switch on as required. One that was very different from the person she was in private. I watched her talk and gesture happily, and I could see Marcello's delight.

"I hope your sister becomes as attached to this place as you are, Maria. And that she will return. I hope to see you both here again soon."

I nodded but said nothing.

It seemed like the walk back was easier for Emma, but

when we stepped inside, she said she wanted to take a rest. I walked upstairs and sat down by the computer.

The third day. I don't know much more about Emma, even though she has told me about Olof. And that she has been ill. But somehow it's still as if she is not really telling. Or perhaps it is me not listening properly. Perhaps I don't want to know. And I am still trying to avoid telling anything much. Not entirely successfully. This and that slips out, things I have not at all intended to tell. I am not sure what Emma wants to hear. If she wants to hear anything at all. Or if she needs to talk more than anything. My dream about Amanda has lingered all day. It might be Emma's presence that affects me.

I stopped typing. And suddenly I couldn't hold back my tears. They took me by surprise, completely. I stood up and walked onto the terrace and pulled the sliding door closed behind me.

And there I was, weeping like a child. It was as if it would never cease. The tears flowed, as did snot. I sobbed uncontrollably.

It took a long while before I calmed down. I sat in one the chairs and pulled my knees toward my chest. Curled up. As if I was trying to comfort myself.

I let my eyes rest on the familiar view. And I thought about my first day there. It is peculiar that you can remember being happy but still be completely unable to evoke the feeling. That's not how it is with grief. The memory of grief is always accompanied by the feeling. I remembered how we stepped inside the house the first time. How we slowly walked upstairs and downstairs, more and more excited. Explored all three floors. And finally ended up here, on the terrace, side by side. And I remembered how deliriously happy I had been. But now the memory brought only sadness.

I must have dozed off because I woke with a start when I heard Emma open the door. She brought coffee and placed the tray with cups and biscuits on the table. Then she pulled her chair into the sun, unfolded it, and stretched out.

"Anna just called."

I looked at her, where she rested, seemingly unconcerned, her face to the sun and her eyes closed.

"I can't remember when she last called. She wants to come home for Christmas. But I haven't given Christmas a thought. It feels distant and unreal. Like something I used to do a long time ago. I don't even know where I will be living then. Or if I will be up to having another Christmas."

I sat up in my chair.

"Are you not still living in Mariefred?"

"Yes, but the house is on the market. Olof has been generous, allowing me to stay on this long. There was so much to deal with when I became ill. I wasn't up to making a decision about where to go, on top of everything else. So he agreed that I could stay for the time being. Olof works in Stockholm now, and he has a flat there. So the house has to be sold. We can't afford to keep it. And I don't want to stay there anyway. I think."

There was a brief silence.

"I don't know what I want. Or, rather, I want nothing. I can't even begin to imagine how my life could evolve. So I can't make any plans at all."

"Perhaps you just need a little more time."

"Or perhaps quite the opposite. Perhaps I should realize that time is precious. That I need to make some decisions. Begin to walk in some direction."

I stood up, poured the coffee, and handed Emma her cup.

"Now I'm afraid I didn't sound encouraging enough, happy enough, when I talked to Anna. I never know with her. How she is. What she really wants from me."

"Do you need to? Isn't it enough that she calls? Think of your feelings for her. Not the feelings you think she might have for you."

I heard the church bells chime, not sure why. It might have been for a wedding or a funeral. Or just ringing in the Sunday. I closed my eyes against the warm afternoon sun and listened to the chiming and realized that for the first time in a very long time I was aware that a weekend was coming up. The sun had moved beyond our chairs and the terrace was in the shade when we finally stood up.

"Perhaps we should go shopping? We promised to bring lunch for the boat trip." Emma walked ahead, toward the steps, tray in her hands. Then she stopped. "And I was going to suggest that I make dinner at home tonight. If that's all right."

༜

Since I ate out more often than not, both my pantry and my fridge were miserably empty. Emma checked them and wrote a list of things we needed to buy.

The fish counter at the small supermarket didn't open until after seven, when the fishing boats returned with the day's catch, so it was almost dark when we set off. We stopped on the way and had a glass of wine. Several of my favorite places had closed for the season, but when people from Barcelona and the inland returned for weekends, some opened again.

"That color suits you." Emma wore a blue linen dress and a matching cardigan. My compliment was honestly intended but she looked skeptical.

"I don't think anything suits me anymore."

"You got some color from the walk today, I think. That suits you too."

I wore the same jeans as before and a similar T-shirt. Nothing much to comment on. And that might have been the intention. Not to be noticed.

Emma regarded me with her head a little cocked, as if assessing me.

"You don't seem to care much what you wear, do you? I admire that. I wish I could ignore it too. But I feel I need to dress with care. Put on makeup. Hide. And when someone makes a kind comment about how I look, I assume they're referring to the clothes, not me. It feels like a pat on the shoulder, an acknowledgment of my efforts, nothing more."

"But I meant you. Not your clothes. You look good in what you are wearing. I'm not sure I would have noticed those garments on someone else. Or in a shop. It's you who look good in them."

To my amazement, she blushed. And turned demonstratively to make contact with the waiter and ask for the bill.

We took our time in the supermarket, and I was surprised at how much fun it was. We talked about what to bring for the boat trip the following day.

"Do you think we'll go ashore somewhere? If so, perhaps we can bring a small grill? If you have one?"

"I don't think it needs to be that elaborate. Some bread, cheese, olives. I think that will do just fine."

We gathered what we needed for the lunch, and then Emma focused on the dinner.

"Is there anything special you would fancy? Or something you don't like?" She gave me a searching look. "I have no idea what you like. I don't remember anything from when we were little. What did we eat?"

I shrugged. "There were times when there wasn't much to eat at all. But that was before your time, I think. After our father had left and before your father came into the picture. Later there was more money. But the food didn't improve very much. In hindsight, I have sometimes wondered if Mother had some kind of eating disorder. I just can't picture her at the table. She used to stand by the counter while we ate. I can picture her there, leaning against the counter with a cigarette in her hand. Funny, I don't usually remember that she smoked. Nor do I remember that she ever seemed to look forward to a meal. I think she would have preferred not to have to be involved at all. That's how it felt. As if it was a chore, never a pleasure. I think both Amanda and I ate to survive. I remember we were often hungry, but not that we enjoyed the food. So when you ask me what I like and what I don't like, I struggle to give you an answer. As you must have noticed, I have most of my meals out. I am hopeless at cooking, but I enjoy other people doing it for me. I'm embarrassed about that. It feels immature somehow. As if I have an unsatisfied need for some kind of care. As if the food is not so much food but a symbol of something else.

But you must have a different view entirely. I remember your lavish dinner parties. How you invited us for Christmas dinner and birthday lunches in your beautiful home. Olof and you. Or was it mostly you?"

Emma shrugged.

"Yes, I guess it was mostly me." Again, she looked at me with a thoughtful expression. "When I listen to you, I wonder if my relationship with food isn't somehow similar. I do like cooking. But it has never really been about the food. It is a way for me to express love, I think. But it wasn't food my family needed. How Olof felt about it, I never knew. I think perhaps he understood that it meant a lot to me. But I don't think he ever understood how to respond to it. I don't think food was anything other than nourishment to him. He never seemed particularly interested. And to expect him to understand how charged it was for me was probably to ask too much. When I put the food on the table, it was really to tell them how much I loved them. But what I did was never enough, never the right thing. Then when Anna became ill, our meals turned into torture. And my efforts only served to make them worse. For me, it was as if she rejected not just the food but my love."

"I had no idea that was how you felt. And I had no idea Anna was ill. I was overwhelmed. Everything was perfect in your home. I just felt I didn't fit in."

Emma walked slowly down the aisle, and I followed.

"I thought I'd make something simple. A salad perhaps," she said without turning around.

And that's what we decided.

⟡

Emma didn't want any help in the kitchen, but I stood on the other side of the island, watching her slice tomatoes. I placed my phone on the counter and connected it to a loudspeaker and turned on some music. We had often listened to music when we first moved in. During evenings on the terrace. In the morning when we had our coffee. And when Maya cooked. That time had its own musical score. I hesitated before I decided what to play now. The time before the music finally flowed forth felt longer than I had anticipated. For a few seconds, I wondered if I had lost the music.

Emma looked up.

"What is this?"

"The singer's name is Arianna Savall, and she sings in Catalan. When I first discovered her, I used to listen to her not just because I thought it was beautiful. I wanted to learn the language too. But nothing much has come of that."

"It's very beautiful, regardless."

Every song brought memories from those early days. But again I was unable to re-create the feeling. Just remember it and allow myself to be filled with immense regret.

"Yes, the music is lovely," I said. "This particular one is called '*Ya salió de la mar*,' which I think means something like 'she came out of the sea.'"

I felt my eyes brim with tears. Again. I sensed Emma's eyes on me and gestured to her to ignore me.

"Don't look at me. It's just been a long time since I heard this."

Emma had made a salad with fresh tuna and plated it elegantly on a dish I hadn't even seen before. She had chilled white wine and water, sliced bread and found a basket for it. We carried everything upstairs to the terrace. The metal table had rusty spots and needed cleaning. Suddenly I remembered that there were tablecloths in a drawer in the kitchen, and I went downstairs to get one. I also found a few tea lights, but I had to search for a while before I found matches in the small cupboard on the wall by the fireplace. It didn't occur to me to ask Emma for her lighter.

It looked inviting when it was ready, and we sat down to eat.

"It's been a long time since I've dined this elegantly."

"You find this elegant? Just a salad and some bread and wine. I've seen far more elegant dinners."

"Oh, that's not what I meant. You can see that someone has made an effort to make this not only tasty but also very beautiful to look at."

Emma served and we began to eat.

"Have you opened the envelope?"

I had completely forgotten. Suppressed it, perhaps. I shook my head.

"I'm sorry if it's difficult. That was never my intention."

"It's not difficult. I just forgot." I put down my cutlery.

"Everything to do with Mother is . . . hard. I just can't do it. I don't want to."

I searched for words, something I could say without releasing all I had worked so hard to hold back.

"When I think back, only sad memories surface."

Emma looked at me. "Don't you remember that she used to sing with us?"

"With us? I do remember her singing. She had such a beautiful voice. What she might have made of it if she had not met Father. And had us, Amanda and me. But I do not remember her singing *with* us. Possibly *to* us. But not much of that either. Besides, I can't sing. So it couldn't have been particularly inspiring to sing with me."

"Do you see everything that one-dimensionally? So darkly?"

"What do you mean? How else should I see it? I think I see it as it was. If you have another picture, it might be because you had, not just another father, but another mother too. We are not the same person in different relationships."

"That's right, of course. But we still lived together, the two of us, for more than ten years. Same place, same mother. Not everything could have been different."

"I don't know, Emma." I searched her face, where the

candlelight chiseled out its features. I had always thought Emma took after Mother. Now I could see that this was just a superficial likeness. The colors, her posture, some gestures. But here, up close, I could see no other similarities at all. Nor could I see any resemblance to the younger sister she had been as a child. It was an unfamiliar face, one I could relate to more easily.

As if she had read my thoughts, she looked up while she too put down her cutlery.

"When I was little, I thought you were so beautiful, Amanda and you. I wanted to be like you, look like you. Once I brushed my hair with Mother's mascara to make it dark. Do you remember? Mother was furious."

I shook my head.

"It was as if everything about you was stronger, healthier. Not just your dark, curly hair. Mine was blonde, almost white, and dead straight. Like Mother's. And your skin was a little tanned even in winter. I just got pink and freckled in the sun and very white in winter. You were made to be out and about, but I was best suited to some dark corner. I just couldn't get enough of watching you. I remember how you used to climb up the tree behind our building, lithe and strong like monkeys. Then you sat up there and watched my awkward attempts to follow. I would stand there, crying, until Amanda took pity on me and came down. But you stayed up there. Always out of reach."

"Out of reach. That's an odd expression when you

consider it. You can look at it from two sides. Who is reaching for whom? I never felt out of reach. It was just that nobody reached out for me. Nobody but Amanda. I have so few memories of my father. A handful of photos, of course. I can see that we looked like him. But I have so few real memories. After he moved out, we only saw him for a week or so during the summer holidays. And then he used to come for a brief visit at Christmas. But they were awkward visits. He was so obviously there to see Mother. And Mother was so obviously not interested. It was a game involving the two of them, really."

"I do remember him, actually. I used to dream that he was really my father too."

"Why? Your father adored you. You were his little princess."

Emma's response took a long while.

"I don't really know what my father felt for me. I have no memories of us doing anything much together. He came and he went. Mostly, he went. That's what it felt like. And when he was home, it was as if we all had to tiptoe around him. I wasn't afraid of him. Not for my sake. But it scared me how our home changed when he was there. It was as if he pulled me away from you. As if I was an object that belonged to him, an object that was useful to him in some way. At his funeral I was all alone. Mother certainly wasn't there. I think she was abroad. She had met Robert by then. And Mother and Father had been divorced for quite some time. There wasn't really any reason for her to be there. Other than for my sake, I suppose. I remember that I cried inconsolably. I have no idea why, because I don't think I grieved for him really. Perhaps I was ashamed of my lack of grief? Or else it was the insight that I was now completely alone."

"Mother was still around."

Emma stared at me as if she wasn't really sure if I was serious.

"Like you said, Mother had left us a long time ago. Perhaps she had never really been present. I have always had a feeling of being conceived as a part of her plan to catch Father. And then, when she lost interest in Father, she lost what little interest she might have had in me."

"At least you were once a wanted child. Not a mistake to be regretted, like Amanda and me."

"I'm not sure. I might have been wanted, in some way. But when nothing turned out the way it was supposed to, I became a burden. A responsibility she didn't want. Sometimes she would look at me with what felt like revulsion. As if there was something wrong with me and I didn't match the expectations that she once had. But that was on the odd occasion when she took any notice of me at all. Mostly, I was invisible. And eventually her restless chase for something else resumed, and I ceased to exist. I agree with you. I don't think she ever found what she was searching for."

I topped up our glasses.

"I have wished I could talk to my father. If only for a little while. Be allowed to ask my questions and hear his answers. Have his version of how it all began. Because I can't for the life of me imagine their love affair. If that is the correct term for our conception, Amanda's and mine. I can't understand how two such ill-matched people could be attracted to each other. But I may not understand anything at all. For neither of them ever said how it was in the beginning. It might have started as love. Perhaps they were happy together for some time. I hope so, but that is not how it feels. Sometimes I watch adult daughters with their fathers, and I envy them so. Actually, I think I longed for my father even as a child. I longed for him to be more present in our lives. I remember that he held me close when we sat in the church at Amanda's funeral. Neither of us wept anymore, but Father kept squeezing my arm hard, again and again. I had no idea then that he was so ill. I have never found out if he knew. But he died just a month later. I thought we had our whole lives ahead of us. That the grief was going to connect us in a new way. Because we were the only ones mourning Amanda like that. We had agreed that I was going to come and live with him. I was just going to finish the term at school, and I had already more or less left home and was living with Olof's family. But when the term ended, Father was no longer there."

"You're saying you were the only two mourning Amanda.

But you are forgetting me," Emma whispered. "I mourned her terribly. And I had nobody at all to share my grief."

She started to collect our plates and cutlery, then she stood up, for a moment looking down at me.

"We have to talk about Amanda. Sometime we have to do that."

I twirled my glass in my hand.

"There is nothing to talk about, Emma."

She didn't reply, just disappeared inside. I thought she would return, but after I had waited a good while I stood up and blew out the candles. I leaned against the banister and looked out over the sea. It was a starry night with strong moonlight. It was late and the sounds were soft, but I could see the odd person still strolling along the quay.

I was wrong. We did need to talk about Amanda.

DAY FOUR

No dreams. None that I could remember anyway. And no lingering feelings. I could tell that it was later than I had intended, but I remained in bed for a little while. I heard discreet sounds from the kitchen downstairs. Emma was up. I registered it as a fact but with no particular reaction. Perhaps I was getting used to her presence.

When I came down the stairs, I could see that she had set the table on the patio, but I couldn't spot her anywhere. I poured myself a cup of coffee and sat down. The metal seat felt cold through my dressing gown. A small bird with a red chest landed at the top of the wall and sat watching me for a while before it lifted and landed in the fig tree a little farther up. There it began to sing. The small body seemed to gather all its strength before each quaver and the downy red chest feathers ruffled up. From where I sat, it looked as if the chest was covered in blood, as if the bird sang with its last strength and at a terrible cost.

I didn't notice Emma until she was right beside me. I looked up and thought she looked better.

"Good morning," she said, and sat down.

"Good morning. You look like you've had a good night." She nodded.

"Yes, it's been a long time since I slept right through an entire night. I woke up early and went for a walk to town and bought bread."

This time I helped myself to a croissant. It was still warm. I tore off a small piece and popped it into my mouth. The little bird sat among the fig leaves, still singing. I stood up and stepped onto the edge of the flower bed. From there, I could just reach the top of the wall if I stretched out my arm. I placed a few breadcrumbs there, sat down again, and pointed to the bird. It took just a moment. We watched it soundlessly sweep down and snatch a crumb, only to disappear among the leaves again.

We smiled and it felt almost genuine.

"What do you say? Shall we walk to Cap de Creus?"

As far as I could judge from the square above us, the sky was absolutely clear. "I think we'll have another fine day."

Emma nodded. "Sounds good. Do what you need to do first. You decide when we leave."

All agreed, I went inside to get ready.

I heard the music inside me. It struck me that it no longer made me sad. There was something more to it. An odd sense of gratitude perhaps. An unfamiliar warmth.

⚜

At a leisurely pace, it would take us just under two hours. It felt as though Emma moved a little lighter, and I had no difficulty adapting my pace to hers. When I walk alone, I don't see the landscape in the same way as I do when I have company. I see it more intensely and at the same time I don't see it at all. Intensely when I take pictures. Or when I stop to enjoy the view. And not at all when my thoughts wander, and I can walk long distances without noticing my surroundings. When startled out of my thoughts, I can feel embarrassed in the same way I used to when I woke up sleepwalking when I was little.

But now I was not alone. I was walking side by side with my sister, and as I adapted my step to hers, I tried to see the landscape as she might see it. I couldn't imagine that she found it beautiful. The barren terrain with sharp rocks and spiky plants couldn't possibly appeal to Emma.

"It's beautiful."

I couldn't help laughing.

"Really?"

"Yes, I think it looks as if it was created only yesterday.

And at the same time it looks ancient. It's as if everything came to a halt in the midst of being created. As if someone just tired of it and left it to its fate."

I let my gaze run over the gray, stony landscape. The sky was blanching in the intense sunlight. A glimpse of sea was visible on the horizon. Emma had described it well. It looked like the enormous land mass had poured forth toward the water and the momentum had abruptly halted while the volcanic melt was spilling into the depths of the sea.

About halfway, we took a break and sat down on a rock a little off the walkway. From there, we had a wide view over the sea.

"I think Pau will take us up this way tomorrow. So you will see it all again but from a different perspective."

Emma had her eyes on the sea.

"It will be very different. Everything depends on perspective."

We had some fruit and water, and Emma offered a few pieces of chocolate, a little melted in the heat.

"How are you feeling? We're at least halfway by now."

"Absolutely fine. It's lovely to be out like this. I had almost forgotten the feeling. Just walking, not having to think at all. Total freedom."

We arrived at our destination just before one. In spite of the fine weather, the restaurant was half empty and we had no problem getting a table in the shade outside.

"It feels as if we are sitting right at the edge of the earth, at the last frontier. As if there is nothing beyond the sea."

I nodded.

"Yes, everything worldly feels distant. That is how I feel when I am in Cadaqués. Alone in the house, I sometimes find myself wondering if the world still exists outside. And even more so out here, of course."

"I can imagine how lonely you might feel in that large house."

I hesitated for moment before I responded.

"It has nothing to do with the house. The truth is that I feel less lonely there than I do anywhere else. I feel safe there."

I imagined Emma couldn't understand what I meant. But she nodded slowly.

"I am not sure if I understand how you feel, but one reason why I haven't sorted my own housing is that I feel safe in my old home. But it is a false sense of security, I have come to understand. No security at all, really. I will have to leave it one day. I am well aware of that. And that day is rapidly approaching. I'm living on borrowed time and no closer to an idea of where to go. Thinking about it makes me panic."

"Yes, perhaps there isn't that much difference between how we live our lives, you and I. My house represents a brief time in my life when I was completely happy. Everything that reminds me of that time is in that house. When I am there by myself I occasionally experience moments when the memory almost comes alive. It might be music. A fragrance. A dream. Or just the view over the sea."

Emma's hands were playing with the napkin, but her thoughts seemed to be elsewhere. Then she looked up.

"But to live like that is not living. You can't live your life backward. Not in the long term. I just don't know how to take a step outside again. I have locked myself inside for so long. I have no memories of the kind of happiness I think you are describing. But all the things I have experienced, I experienced there, in my home. I can look backward, but when I try to look forward, I see nothing. And that is so terribly frightening."

"I still think you may have gotten further than I have. That your insight is greater. That you may already have taken the first step. You are just not aware of it. But I, I have nothing pulling me. Nothing that forces me to pick up my life again. I can stay hidden here in my house."

It looked like Emma started to say something, then changed her mind.

"You have told me so much about yourself, Emma. About Olof and the children. But I have given you hardly anything."

"You don't have to tell me anything. What I have told you, I told you for my sake. Not yours. I needed to talk about Olof. It's as if one sees things more clearly when one tries to put them into words. It has been so lonely carrying this sad story of the divorce. So look at it as my self-therapy. It comes with no obligation to reciprocate."

A fleeting, slightly self-conscious smile touched her lips before she took a sip of wine.

"To me, telling is certainly no therapy. I think I carry my sad story around because I don't want to put it down. It is all I have, and I don't know how I would be able to live without it surrounding me all the time. I was afraid before your arrival. Afraid and furious. I didn't want to share any part of my small world with anyone else. I have inhabited it for a year now. At first I didn't leave the house for days. And all this time I haven't invited anyone inside."

I couldn't understand what it was I was doing. But I placed my glass on the table and met Emma's eyes.

"When I stood there, after the funeral, and invited you here, I regretted it the moment the words popped out of my mouth. I had no idea why I uttered them. But when I thought about it the other day, I realized it was hubris, quite simply. Do you remember that Mother used to say you should be careful showing that you are happy? Even to yourself? That to do so is to challenge fate?"

Emma nodded.

"Yes, I do remember. But I absolutely do not believe it. I think it's a terrible thought. For most people, there is so little happiness that surely you must be allowed to embrace it?"

"Yes, that makes sense. But I cannot shake the feeling

Mother planted in me. I think I have held back all my life. Been careful not to show real happiness. Real love. Well, feelings generally. But at that moment when I invited you here, I refused to listen to Mother's warning. I really wanted to show how happy I was. I wanted you to know. Perhaps particularly you. I wanted to share it with you."

"Why me? You keep saying we hardly know each other."

I shrugged. "I can't explain. An indication of my arrogance, I suppose. Completely stupid. And I knew it instantly. But it would be a year before fate caught up with me."

The waiter appeared and we ordered coffee.

"When you told me how you felt when you met Olof, I realized that it had no likeness to my feelings for him. To me, he was really just a friend. A steadfast and loyal friend. And I escaped into that security when everything collapsed at home. But Olof opened no doors for me. He blocked them. Suffocated me with his love. I wanted to live! It felt like my life hadn't even started yet. And I could see nothing beyond Olof as long as he was close to me. He closed all roads, blocked all exits. When I looked at him, all I could see were his expectations. Expectations that I knew I would not be able to live up to. Eventually, I couldn't stand looking at him."

I regarded Emma for a moment and then took a deep breath.

"Then I got pregnant. And my whole world fell apart.

Olof was my only confidant. But this I could never share with him. Not with anybody. I knew I would never be able to make Olof understand. I had reached the point where I had to leave. So I had an abortion. And then I went to London. But you know that."

I felt as if I was in free-fall. As if I had taken a leap, not knowing when I would gain a foothold again.

"I don't know why I am telling you this. It's not what I had in mind to say. But I suppose there is a kind of connection somehow. What I wanted to try to explain was what happened between my invitation and your e-mail. Two years."

"You don't owe me any explanations," Emma said. "Shall we move over there? Go and sit in the sun? It's getting a little chilly here."

We paid and left our table. The view was spectacular now that the sun sat lower in the sky. Where the enormous, rugged rocks met the sea, the water was intensely turquoise, shifting into deep blue farther out.

"But I really do want to tell. I need to."

Did I really want to? And if so, why? Did I feel like Emma, that I wanted to put something into words to see it more clearly? No, certainly not. I did see it absolutely clearly. So why did I suddenly have this urge to put my most precious memories into words? Take the risk that words would damage what I cherished most? It made no sense. But I continued.

"I came here by chance the first time. I wasn't headed here but had planned to stay in Roses. But then I fell asleep on the bus and ended up at the last station. In Cadaqués. When I stepped off, I knew immediately that this was mine. That is so very unlike me. I see myself as a realistic, logical person, not prone to anything esoteric. But this place and me, we were meant for each other. I knew it. Behind every corner I found exactly what I had expected. It was autumn then too. But not as late as now. There were still some tourists around, but it was already strangely tranquil. I had been to Barcelona for an interview with the school that I ended up working at. My life seemed to have come to a standstill, allowing me to look around and consider my options. And make a new start, I guess. I had lived in London all those years. But now I was single again. I didn't find the house then. That happened later. After I had met Maya. I moved to Barcelona a few months later and started at the school at the beginning of the year."

I hesitated, not sure how to continue.

"At first I rented an apartment for a few weeks. While I searched for a place of my own. The school had arranged the rental, and I had never met the owners. But it was clear that they were into art. The place was filled with interesting paintings. When the agreed weeks ended, I had found an apartment of my own. My landlords, Raul and Agnés, returned, and when we met, they invited me to Raul's upcoming vernissage. The art in their place was all

Raul's, and the exhibition was a show of his latest works. I knew nothing about art then. Not that I know much now, either. But I liked his work. Large canvases, strong colors, stark and a little challenging, but with lots of details to discover if you looked closer. We arrived early, and I was introduced to the owner of the gallery, Maya."

I threw Emma a quick glance. Perhaps to check if she was listening. She sat with her face turned to the sun and her eyes hidden behind her sunglasses.

"My life hasn't contained that much love. Or what you might call intimate relationships. Sex. Romance. My longest relationship lasted six years. And as you know, I have no children.

"I can honestly say that I have never allowed myself to be swept away in some kind of uncontrollable attraction. Apart from Elliot, there were a couple of relationships I might have wished had lasted. But not until I met Maya did I understand what it feels like to really love."

I stopped and waited until she turned her face to me.

"So I didn't have a husband in my house, Emma. I had Maya."

Again it looked as if Emma started to speak, and then changed her mind.

"And when I met you at Mother's funeral, we had just found our house here. We were waiting to see if we would be able to buy it, but at first we rented it for nine months. The duration of a pregnancy, and perhaps that is how we saw it. Time for us to plan our future. Something like that. We drove here for holidays and often just for weekends. Maya had known Pau for many years. He was also one of her artists and regularly exhibited at her gallery. And it was Pau who told us about the house. During that early period, we spent a lot of time together, the three of us. Pau has his studio in his family home and spends more time here than in Barcelona. When I think about that time now, I understand that it was too good to last. Too much happiness. Too much love. Now I can hear Mother's voice loud and clear. But then I felt invincible. I paraded my love everywhere. And I think Maya felt the same. We were totally absorbed by our unexpected love, and we neither saw nor heard anything else. I'm not sure if Maya ever understood how extraordinary it was for me. How little I had experienced before. But I believe she realized how infinitely happy I was."

The sun had disappeared behind the restaurant, and with it the warmth.

"Shall we begin our walk back?"

Emma nodded and we stood up.

After a little while she slowed in her tracks and turned toward me.

"It is so utterly sad that neither of us seems to feel we deserved the love that we were given."

"Oh, I think I did then. I did think I deserved it. Then. It's only in hindsight that I look at myself and think I was so ridiculously cocky. So absolutely confident that I deserved it all. I saw an endless future exactly the same as the present. An absurd thought that you only believe when you are deliriously in love. Come to think of it, deep grief might affect one in the same way. You can see no end to it ever. Something that completely overpowers you, good or bad, does that. Distorts your perspective. Makes you unable to see beyond the present. Time stops and you believe everything is permanent. But neither joy nor grief lasts forever. Sometimes you come across people who have lived a long life together and still seem to love each other sincerely. But it doesn't happen often. And I don't believe that even those people live in an eternal, hot passion. So even if we had been granted what we were hoping for, Maya and I, a long life together, we wouldn't have lived forever in that initial, overwhelming love. It would have evolved into something else. But as things turned out, all I can envision is what we had when it ended. And that's why the pain is still unbearable."

We started to walk again, and when Emma made no comment, I continued.

"I can't remember that I have ever before experienced what you described when you told me about your feelings for Olof. A sudden, intense love, impossible to suppress or control. And lasting. All my previous relationships now seem so . . . well, trivial. I suppose I have to call Olof my first adult love, even though we were very young. But it seemed more as if he stepped into my life without an invitation, as such, and just made himself comfortable. And he always seemed to be waiting for something I couldn't possibly give him. Considerate and clever. Funny sometimes. I suppose I thought that was all I needed. Or all I deserved. And I liked to have him around, mostly. At least initially. But all the time there was that awkward irritation lurking just below the surface. Because I was also waiting for something I now understand Olof was unable to give."

Suddenly I no longer felt sure how much more I wanted to tell. I looked at Emma, but she seemed absorbed by her own thoughts. "You said it was as if Olof opened the door to the world for you. I might describe my entering Maya's world in the same way. I am a teacher. I love my job. I believe I am good at it. But I have almost always worked in international schools. With motivated students and engaged parents. A protected world in many ways. I suppose there is an element of creativity in teaching, but for me much of it has become routine. Apart from the fact that the students are new each year. But in Maya's world nothing at all seemed routine. She was a very good businesswoman in a competitive line of work. What drove her wasn't the business itself but the creative aspect of it. It took a while before I realized that she was a talented artist herself. But she regarded her own art as a source of inspiration only. Something very private. I think what she enjoyed the most was the search for talent. Especially young, new talent.

And she was very good at it. Proud, too, of the artists she had discovered over the years. Now, when I tell you this I realize that perhaps there wasn't that great a difference between our jobs. I am also immensely proud of my students who have continued to study languages and literature. And perhaps that is the aspect of my job I love most. The discovery of ability, or perhaps, rather, being able to inspire interest and nurture proficiency in a young person. Especially so when it happens unexpectedly. But Maya's world still felt so much more exciting than mine. I really don't know what she thought about mine. Somehow her world took over. Partly because I wanted to be there, partly because we were able to share hers, while mine largely remained my own. I wasn't really able to bring Maya along to my school, but I came to spend a lot of time at the gallery. And then . . . well, now the gallery is mine, even though I'm not really involved in the daily running of it. The day when I have to decide is rapidly approaching. I will have to make up my mind what to do. About everything."

Suddenly Emma placed her hand lightly on my arm and pointed to the sky. A large flock of small black birds moved with grace across the blue expanse, separating into smaller flocks, only to unite again. Spreading out and contracting in a pattern that looked almost choreographed.

"Here they are called *estornells*, those little black birds. I think they are starlings. I have never seen them behave like this anywhere else. Only here. But that might be because I was never really interested in birds before I came here. I have never really felt a part of nature in the sense that I do here. Even here the feeling is fleeting and unpredictable. But watching these birds I am overcome with a sense of belonging."

I cringed at my own words. It sounded ridiculous. But it was true. We stood side by side, watching the birds for quite a while.

"You can't even tell that they are individual birds. It's like one homogenous body. Like ballet in the sky. Or a mobile work of art. Strange and alluring." Emma raised her hand as if tracing the flight of the birds.

"We used to walk here, Maya and I. It was neutral ground for us. Something to discover together. As with the house. It was our only shared home. In Barcelona we kept our respective homes. At least for the time being that was the idea, until we made a decision about the house. But it was only here that we were truly together. So it really is rather odd that I linger here alone. When nothing is as before and I no longer feel connected to anything. I might be clinging to this in order not to lose my memories. Perhaps I have built myself a shrine here."

We reached the place where we had rested earlier, and we climbed up the rock again. Emma sat down, but I remained standing, looking out over the sea. Without really taking in any of what lay before me.

"We were planning to have our first Christmas here.

My holidays had already started, so we agreed that I would drive here and prepare things. We had invited a few friends, people we knew well and liked, including Raul and Agnés. And Pau, even though he wasn't going to stay with us, of course. It was always Maya who did the cooking; I was just an assistant. You know how hopelessly bad I am at cooking. But she had given me lists of things to buy and things to do and prepare. And she had packed several boxes of glassware and crockery. 'At Christmas you can't use other people's plates,' she said, laughing. We got everything into the car and then she held me tightly. 'Drive carefully, Mariona,' she said, and kissed me three times, once on each cheek and lastly on my mouth. Then she tucked my hair behind my ears and looked me in the eyes. In a way, this gesture meant more to me than the kisses. Nobody had ever done that with my hair. But Maya often did."

I still stood with my back to Emma, and I wasn't sure whether she could hear me. But it no longer mattered.

"You know what the road is like. How steep it is. And how very winding. And Maya left so late. There was a lot to do before she could leave for the holiday. She was to go with Raul and Agnés in their car. 'Don't stay up and wait for me,' she said. As if I would be able to sleep before she had arrived."

There was no turning back now. So I continued.

"She called me when they were getting ready to leave Barcelona. Sometimes the reception is poor on the road down to Cadaqués, and I didn't expect her to call again. So it was quite some time before I began to worry. I told myself they must have left later than they had planned. That something had delayed them at the last minute. Or that they had stayed somewhere on the way. I sat upstairs, on the terrace, and waited. First, in the warm anticipation you experience when you wait for someone you love. Then with the concern you have only for someone you love. The hours went by. I told myself there were lots of perfectly natural explanations for the delay. I tried calling Maya's phone again and again, but I only got the voice mail. I called both Raul's mobile and Agnés's but got no reply. So I was immensely relieved when there was finally a loud knock on the door, and I dashed downstairs. But it wasn't Maya. It was Pau."

Now I wept. But I ignored my tears. And I remained where I was, with my back to Emma.

"They died, all three of them. Agnés lived for two days, but we knew she wasn't going to make it. Maya and Raul had died instantly. The police suspected that an animal had crossed the road. And Raul had swerved and lost control. They were so close, just another ten minutes and they would have been here."

When I fell silent, I heard the sea far below. And seabirds high above.

"Come and sit here," Emma said after a while, and I turned. I wept and wept. It felt as if I had never really wept like this before.

"Come."

We sat like that for a long time. Side by side, with no need to say anything at all.

"Pau stayed all night. He sat with me and held me as long as I needed it. And when I finally fell asleep, I knew he was still there beside me. In the morning he took care of everything. Took me where I had to go. Made all the phone calls. And made innumerable cups of coffee and placed food in front of me. That is why it's so very difficult for me to have him in my house now."

They poured out, things I hadn't even been aware of carrying.

"When I see him, I only see his pity. Yet I know that he has his own grief. Raul was one of his best friends. They had known each other since they were teenagers and they went to art school together. Pau was best man when Raul and Agnés married. And I know he loved Maya almost as much as I did. He might feel the same as I do. I don't know. For a long time I never even considered his grief. When you are in deep mourning, you become so very selfish. Perhaps we remind each other too much of our grief, Pau and I. Or else he keeps the distance only out of respect for me. Nowadays we only exchange a few words when we meet."

Emma made no comment. It was as if she gave me time to collect myself. And I was immensely grateful.

Eventually, we stood up and carried on home.

❧

It was late afternoon, and I was sitting on the terrace. Emma had withdrawn to her room when we returned. I had no regrets. Unlike earlier instances in my life when I had told things in confidence, I didn't dwell on what I had said. I wasn't worried about how my words had fallen, or what impression I might have made. It struck me that I felt relieved. Perhaps it was just as Emma had said. Not a sharing of secrets at all. Perhaps I was finally expressing in words what I had dreaded confronting. I had in no way diminished it. Or distorted it. Or destroyed it. Everything I carried was still there. Clearer than ever. And I was relieved. It had been hard. But not as hard as I had thought.

We had made no plans for the evening. I wasn't particularly hungry. But I went downstairs to check the fridge. The house was still silent, and I tried to move carefully, so as not to disturb Emma. But I hardly made it down the stairs, and she opened her door.

"I didn't wake you, did I?"

She shook her head. "I haven't slept. Just rested a little. I have discovered that I can let my body rest without sleeping. It has made a difference. I used to worry about my difficulties with sleep. For long periods I took sleeping pills. But they didn't really help. I used to be tired all day. Now I am more rested, even if I haven't slept that much."

She smiled, and again I thought I saw a glimpse of the young Emma.

"There isn't much to make a meal of here," I said, peering into the fridge. "Shall we go out? It doesn't need to be late or fancy. There are lots of small places nearby."

And it was decided.

It was still rather early and not many people were out. We chose a small restaurant in town. It felt like we were both occupied by our own thoughts, and we didn't talk much. But the silence was not at all awkward.

When we finished the main course, Emma suddenly set down her glass.

"Why are you so sure you know what other people think, Maria?"

She cocked her head and looked at me as if she was genuinely interested in my response.

I shrugged. "Am I?"

"You keep saying you do. You said you knew what Mother was thinking. During all those years when you hardly saw her at all. And you knew precious little about her life. And today you said that Pau just pities you. How do you know that?"

"I guess it's something I just feel."

"Is that really enough to go on, do you think? Have you never thought that you have been wrong? Heard someone describe a situation after the fact and become

111

aware of how you have misconstrued everything? How can you always be so sure of everything? In spite of taking so little interest in other people?"

"Why do you think I have little interest in other people?"

"It's not me thinking! It's you saying. And you show it often. All these years when you never once got in touch with us. Did you never wonder how we were? Did you never think of us?"

"Did you think of me? Nobody got in touch with me either. It was as if I had no family. Besides, what do you know about my life? Did you ever give me a thought? Wonder if I was lonely? If I was homesick? If I wished that someone would be interested enough to find out if I was still alive? You have no idea."

Emma leaned forward.

"You're doing it again! Presuming you know what I was thinking. Or, rather, not thinking. It was you who left us! And I have told you how terribly I missed you. That I hardly knew how to survive your departure. You have no idea what became of our home. And how lonely I was."

"I hear you. But I never felt that I meant anything at all to you. Or that I had any responsibility for you. You were not my child. You were my half sister. And I hardly knew you. I felt no connection with you. Not with anybody else either, for that matter. Not after I lost Amanda."

"But to me it was the other way around! When Amanda

was not there anymore, I needed you even more. Not just in a practical sense. But to share the grief. For me, you were a part of Amanda. Her mirror image. And I tried every way I knew to make you see me. Not in the same way as Amanda had, perhaps, but in some way. Any way. My grief was completely overwhelming. I didn't know how I would be able to live with it. And I wanted to comfort you too. I wanted us to hold each other up. But you turned your back on me. And left."

I met Emma's gaze and thought I could see how she pleaded. How she wanted something from me.

"I was ten years old when you disappeared from my life." She said it so quietly I could hardly hear. But I knew what she was saying. And suddenly the memories washed over me. I remembered her childish eyes then. Her quietly pleading looks. And I remembered avoiding them. I had not known then what to do with them, and I didn't know now either.

"I cannot share, Emma. I have no idea how to. For me, sharing only means losing. Never gaining. To see you, really see you, would have been intolerable for me. It would have made it impossible for me to carry on. It was only by leaving that I was able to keep Amanda inside me. Because when I saw you, I only saw Amanda's absence. It was only ever with Amanda that I was able to share without losing. But I could never share her."

"But Amanda didn't share everything with you, Maria."

"We shared *everything*. That's just how it was with us.

Always. We knew each other inside and out. I don't think you can understand what it was like."

Emma slowly shook her head.

"You never know everything about another person."

"That's how it was with us, anyway."

"We have to talk about Amanda, Maria. We have to do that before it's too late."

"Isn't that what we are doing? Talking about Amanda?" Suddenly I felt nauseous and pushed my plate away. Emma shook her head again.

"Not the way I mean. We need to talk about Amanda's death."

I stood up. "Excuse me. I need to go to the toilet."

I walked through the now almost full restaurant and felt a strong impulse to just carry on and leave. Walk until all thoughts had been extinguished. Until I recovered the peace I had fought so hard to create. But I didn't.

I went to the bathroom and stood in front of the stained mirror and looked at myself while I let the cold water run over my hands.

Maya had said almost the same as Emma. *"Don't assume that people think the way you think they do, Maria. We humans are mysteries, and often we don't even know our own thoughts. We rationalize after the fact. We reinterpret. We misunderstand. We engage in wishful thinking. Actually, it is more important to try to understand your own thinking than to speculate about what others might be thinking. It is never particularly meaningful to plant thoughts in other people's brains. Let them keep their thoughts. It is more important to understand yourself. And difficult enough."* And the way she expressed it, it made sense. I had never felt the need to try and envisage what Maya might be thinking. Because I knew that she loved me.

I stared at my image in the mirror.

What had I really known about Maya's innermost thoughts?

Suddenly I realized that the only thing about Maya I was entirely certain of was that *I* had loved *her*. And I had loved with such trust. My love had been so absolute I had been prepared to fight for it. Die for it.

I realized it had never been like that with Amanda.

Amanda was me. The other half of everything that was me. I had taken her for granted, just like I did myself. But I had not loved her the way you love another person. I had loved her like myself.

I slowly dried my hands under the humming fan.

When I returned to our table, Emma was gone. The waiter noticed my surprise and approached.

"Your friend had to leave. She asked me to give her apologies. And she has paid." I thanked him and left.

I began to walk back. But then I stopped and hesitated for a moment. Emma had her own key, and I supposed that she had left because she wanted to be left alone. So I turned and walked toward the cathedral. Just as I reached the entrance, the door opened and an older man stepped out. He smiled and asked if I was on my way in. He spoke Spanish, not Catalan, so I assumed one could still tell that I didn't quite look like a local. I nodded.

"I'm about to lock up, but if it is important, I can give you a moment. I'll have a cigarette and wait out here."

I thanked him and walked inside.

A few faint and flickering lights were lit at the altar, but it was darker than usual. I walked over to the stand with praying candles, slid a coin into the box, and lit a couple of candles. I had no prayers, and if I had been asked to explain my thoughts, I would have struggled. Why had I come here instead of following Emma back to the house? I assumed that was where she had gone. I sat down in one the pews close to the exit. And as always I tried to step out of my conscious self. If only for a brief moment, it would have felt liberating. But now it was impossible. My own company was too insistent, more so than ever. It obscured everything. I stood up after just a little while.

When I passed the candles, I realized I had come here for my own sake. To say the prayer I was unable to verbalize.

I found the old man standing against the wall outside. When he heard my steps, he turned around.

"I hope you found what you were looking for." He gave me a kind smile.

"Oh, what I am looking for is hard to find."

"But perhaps the moment inside was of some help?"

"It usually helps. But it was hard today."

"It's only when you have tackled the hard bits that it gets easier. And you should never underestimate the value of getting far enough to understand that you are looking for something. It is a good beginning."

"You may be right," I said, and thanked him.

I walked through the narrow alleyways, down to the waterfront, and then carried on slowly along the quay. There was no wind, and the waves lapped softly against the stone wall. It had been a long day. We should never have started to talk about Amanda. It was too late. Not just too late today, but too late in every way. What there was to say should have been said a long time ago.

I crossed the road to walk up to the house, when I heard Emma call my name. At first I wasn't sure from which direction the sound came, but then I noticed her sitting on the bench under the one tree in the small square just where you turn to walk up to the house. She was alone in the darkness.

"I was on my way home, but then I realized I hadn't brought my key."

"Oh, I'm so sorry. I was sure you had it with you. And I thought perhaps you wanted to be left alone. So I went for a walk."

"Come and sit here for a moment."

I sat down, and she placed her hand on my arm. Her fingers were very cold.

"Are you cold?"

She made no reply, just pulled back her hand and stuck it underneath her shawl.

"I want to apologize."

"What for?"

"I shouldn't have started talking about Amanda."

I wasn't sure what to say. I wasn't really sure of my own thoughts. I didn't want to talk about Amanda. I didn't think I wanted to talk about Amanda. But I was no longer certain what I wanted or didn't want.

"One of my earliest memories of Amanda is us sitting at the kitchen table pulling faces at each other."

The moment I began to talk I could see it in my mind. And the feelings were the same as then, the sense of absolute comfort that comes from knowing that someone else understands you absolutely.

"We didn't talk. We were just pulling faces. And we could read each other absolutely. Amanda could lower an eyelid a millimeter or two. Stick out her lower lip. Turn her face a touch. Or just look at me. And I knew exactly what she was thinking. Or at least what she wanted to communicate. I thought that meant I knew what she was thinking. And I remember the immense satisfaction of knowing that she understood me perfectly. Sometimes we would complete each other's sentences. She would finish mine, or I hers. But now I remember other occasions too. When I did not understand her at all. Like when she wanted a red velvet dress for Christmas one year, and Mother wanted to buy us one each. We were little, perhaps five or six. But I wanted a blue and white sailor's dress I had seen in the shop window. And I remember that I felt both triumphant and ashamed when I got it. As if I had somehow failed Amanda. But when I look back on the incident now, I can see that she was not in the least concerned about my choice. She might even have been pleased about having the red dress to herself. It's perfectly possible. I might have been the only one feeling awkward. But the major change, the one that came to stand between us forever, was you, Emma."

"Are you sure it was me? Perhaps I meant less than you think. Perhaps I was less important than the red dress."

I shook my head.

"No. Amanda loved you, Emma. At first I thought she loved the idea of you. A little baby. A living doll."

I heard Emma's short laughter.

"But then she came to love you as a person. And then there was something else."

"Yes?"

"I think she loved the responsibility. She had a defined role in our family—if that is what we were—and it was hers entirely. And it was an important one. She was your mother, really, however young she was. And so she became visible to Mother, I think. Amanda relieved Mother. Not that Mother expressed any gratitude. Ever. But still. And perhaps she was acknowledged even by your father. It was as if she became a part of you. Or perhaps the other way around. Amanda became a little mother. You two came to share a bedroom, while I had my own. I was outside. To you he just said good night on the threshold. But my room he entered and pulled the door closed behind him. More evenings than not. In order to 'say good night.' It was disgusting. He never did anything more than grope, but I dreaded it."

"So perhaps I was something entirely different. Perhaps I was just something for Amanda to hide behind."

"You know that is wrong, Emma. Amanda never hid. She never pretended anything. And I am not sure if she knew how it was for me. I never told anyone. Not even Amanda. Or especially not Amanda. And not Mother. Because I was sure she knew."

I caught Emma's gaze.

"But you knew, didn't you? When you came pattering into my room long after we should all have been asleep. And just stood there."

Emma nodded.

"I just knew that you were sad. And I always hoped that you would turn around and look at me. Even lift the blanket and let me lie down beside you. But you never turned. Even though I always knew you were awake."

I stretched out my hand and placed it gently on her arm. That was all I could manage.

"Perhaps you idealize Amanda? And perhaps you are wrong about Mother?"

Did I? But if Amanda was a part of me, did it mean I idealized myself? Or had I perceived Amanda as the good part and myself as the bad part of the same person? What about Mother, then? What did she really know? What did she think? The absolute certainties I had lived with for all those years seemed to slowly dissolve. Everything lost its sharpness, and I could no longer see clearly. Or think clearly.

"I just don't know. It's cold. I am sure you are freezing. Let's go home."

I had planned to go to bed. Or go and sit on the terrace by myself for a while. But Emma came upstairs with me. It felt cooler than previous evenings, so we sat down on the sofas inside but left the sliding doors open.

"Thank you for a very nice day."

"Thank you. It's been a long time since I walked to Cap de Creus. I have avoided it. But now I can return anytime."

"Only two days left here for me. I was thinking I might try and book a taxi instead of catching the bus. Perhaps Pau can help?"

They would soon be over, these days I had dreaded so. The house would again be mine. The stillness would return. But I could take no comfort from the notion. Nor any relief.

"Tell me about Maya."

Despite its being a perfectly natural request given what I had told her before, I was completely unprepared for the question.

I stood up and stood in the doorway, and looked into the darkness beyond. With my back toward Emma, I had a moment to consider what to say. I wasn't sure I was prepared to share anything more. Then I turned and went to collect the little box that sat on the floor by the sofa.

"It's all in here," I said, and placed the box on the table. "These are my tangible mementos of Maya."

I took out the photos and placed them on the table one by one. There weren't many, and they easily fit beside one another.

Emma sank down from the sofa and kneeled by the low table. She carefully picked up one photo. Looked at it and returned it. When she had looked at them all, she sat back on the sofa again.

"I wish I had met her."

I couldn't look at her. I was sure I would weep again if I met her eyes. So I stood up again and walked out on the terrace. I heard Emma follow.

"Why didn't she come with you to the funeral?"

"I don't know, Emma. Perhaps I was scared."

"Scared?"

I faced her.

"Yes. Scared. There was always a sense of envy at home. A mean and ugly kind of jealousy. It was ever-present, in small matters and in big matters. It was as if even the slightest happiness had to be destroyed. It wasn't just that Mother so often said you mustn't challenge fate and allow yourself to be happy. It was as if she was the judge. The one who decided if you were too happy to be allowed entry. Belonging required a major sacrifice. Enter here only after abandoning love, confidence, happiness, every little success. Only when I was decidedly unhappy could I make myself believe for a moment that I had Mother's approval. Or at least a brief moment of her interest. We both knew how little to expect, didn't we? And what to give up in order to be noticed for a moment. I know, Mother was no longer there, but in some way it felt as if she could still exercise her tremendous influence. And I didn't want to be forced to choose between my love and my family. I wanted to keep Maya away from it. I think it was similar with Elliot. Although we were together for almost six years, I never introduced him to Mother. Or to you. But I cared so much more for Maya."

"I haven't really understood it before. But now, when you describe it, I can see it. Because I always felt that what Mother gave me, she gave me as a reward for my weakness. You remember how often I was sick as a child, don't you? I never felt more accepted than when I was sick. But my successes . . . Well, they haven't been many or notable, but I do remember Mother's lack of interest. The one time I was chosen to be the Lucia at school, she wasn't there. I stood with my eyes on the entrance, candle wax dripping into my hair. I hoped to spot her. I hoped she was just a little late. But she never came. And like I said, more often I was a victim. Sickly, vulnerable, easily frightened, and insecure. I longed infinitely for every crumb of love, and I was prepared to do almost anything for it."

Emma looked at me again with that pleading expression that was so hard for me to handle.

"I needed you. Because you were strong. You resisted. And you know what? I think this scared Mother somehow."

The idea was so absurd I couldn't help but laugh a little.

"There was no need for you to be frightened. I would have welcomed Maya. You would both have been safe. But it was never really about me, was it? It was always only about Mother."

Now I noticed that she was still holding one of the photographs. She regarded it thoughtfully.

"You look a little alike, you and Maya."

I reached out for the photo. I remembered when it had been taken. Maya was standing outside the gallery, in Enric Granados. She had just had the new sign delivered and was pointing at it: MA. *M* for Maya and *A* for art. I remembered she said we would have to replace it when I decided to leave the school and become involved with the gallery.

"We'll have to add another M and it will become MMA." I think that was the first and only time she mentioned that she hoped I would come to work there.

"She is standing outside her gallery in Barcelona. The sign has just been fitted. It was such a happy day. Well, one of many happy days. You can tell, can't you?" I wondered briefly if it was obvious only to me. "I don't think I have that ability. To look happy, I mean. Not even when I am. Mother's voice again, I suppose. But Maya's happiness was generously on display for everybody to see. And I just couldn't get enough of it."

"Well, I think you look alike." She smiled, and I couldn't help but be affected.

"Maya had a kind of deep joy inside her, Emma. Even when she was serious. She couldn't shake it off. It affected everything in her life. It was intoxicating to be in her presence. The world suddenly looked different and infinitely more hopeful."

Unable to continue, I stood up and walked outside. I took in the view of the sea below. The town's lights threw slanted, glittering shafts of light over the mottled black surface. I watched, and I could see all the previous evenings when I had been standing just like this. The warm, happy evenings. They hung like pearls on a string, the first ones shimmering bright, the later ones giving off a flickering faint light.

I heard Emma call my name softly and I returned inside. We sat down on the sofas again.

"I have thought so much about that moment. When we stood there, clearing up after the funeral, and I invited you to come here. I have wondered where the impulse came from. I had not been aware of any such plans. I just wanted the funeral to be over and to return here and never again have to be reminded of anything to do with Mother. But it just slipped out of me. I've wondered if I wanted you to see how happy I was. How I lived here. Well, showing off my life with Maya. That is what I have been thinking. But I am no longer sure."

Emma had pulled up her feet and covered her legs with one of the blankets.

"So what are you thinking now?"

"I regretted the invitation the instant it came out of my mouth. I couldn't understand what had gotten into me. Because I really didn't want you here. And then, well, when I didn't hear from you, I forgot the whole thing. Never gave it another thought."

Emma smiled.

"Yes, I think I realized that was the case. But I just couldn't forget it. It stayed with me. It was something comforting to hold on to while my existence crumbled around me. When nothing else remained, well, I still had you. And your invitation. And for once I didn't care to try to imagine how you would react when you received my e-mail. You had invited me, hadn't you? So I swallowed my pride. Because I really wanted to see you. I needed it. You may not understand how important it was to me. But if you had not replied, or had said no, then I wouldn't have insisted, of course."

I looked at my sister for an extended moment. She

looked small huddled up underneath the blanket. In the dim light, she looked touchingly young but simultaneously ancient. It was as if I could see her entire life span.

"I think you would have liked Maya."

I hesitated, not sure how to express myself. Or rather not quite sure of my own feelings. My thoughts seemed to emerge in that instant, slowly, one at a time. And I allowed the words to follow when I was able to put them into sentences.

"And I think Maya would have liked you. I think now that this is what I sensed at that moment when I invited you to come and visit. I stood and watched you. I could see how tired you were. I was grateful, too, for all that you had taken on. And I was relieved. It was over. It was just the two of us left. You and me. And I wanted you to know that I was no longer afraid of being happy. That I felt I had a right to my love. And I think I wanted you to see me like that, happy. See my real, loving self."

I had held back the tears for such a long while, but now I wept again. It was incomprehensible that I contained all these tears.

"I think I asked to come because I always knew you had it in you, Maria. And I would have given anything to see you happy."

I made a feeble, helpless gesture to indicate that I couldn't speak. Then I stood and walked outside again. I closed my eyes and took deep breaths, but it was as if I was expelling a lifetime of tears. It took me a long while to compose myself.

Emma still sat as I had left her when I returned inside.

"I want to explain to you how it was. How I came to love Maya."

"You don't have to explain anything. I can see how much you loved her."

"But I want to. I want you to understand."

I took a moment to think about what I wanted to say. Wondered why it felt so important. Again, I felt as if I was searching for words to explain my thoughts to myself as much as to Emma.

"I have never sought relationships. It has never bothered me to be alone. Yes, it's hard now. But it's not really hard to be alone. It's not the solitude as such. What is hard is living without Maya. Earlier in my life I lived by myself for long periods. Perhaps it has to do with losing Amanda. The loneliness that came over me then I have lived with ever since. I think it became part of my personality. Part of who I am. And the relationships I have had never really affected that. Even in good relationships I have been lonely. I lived like that with Elliot for six years. Alone but in a relationship."

It sounded extraordinary when I heard myself say it. Six years and we had hardly ever talked about my family. I had told him about Amanda. But I am not sure I even mentioned Emma. And Elliot never seemed particularly interested. On one occasion we did talk about going to Sweden and possibly meeting my family. But that trip never happened. And shortly after, we separated.

"It feels strange now that he never got to meet either of you. Not you and not Mother. I am not sure exactly how I pictured us. Perhaps I never really saw him as a lasting part of my life. I am not sure I ever thought we were going to marry. Have children. We lived together. We had a good life in every way. I think I was happy, as happy as I was capable of being then. We had common interests. He was a professor of Romance languages. We enjoyed traveling together. I wasn't aware of wanting to change anything. And it wasn't me who ended it, not really. Or perhaps it was, in a way. Because, just like Olof, Elliot eventually wanted more than I was able to give him. Above all, he wanted children. It wasn't that he ever made any demands. But I watched him with other people's children. Especially with his sister's three. Occasionally he would talk about it, in general terms. But I knew exactly what he was thinking. What he was hoping. And I realized I couldn't envisage ever being able to give him what he was hoping for. From that moment, our relationship was doomed. We sat on a bench in Regent's Park. It was an early summer afternoon. In front of us, the water was like a mirror and the warm air carried the fragrance of spring flowers. An afternoon filled with immense promise. Made for love and happiness. But we sat there struggling through a conversation that should have happened much earlier. We were both crying. When we walked back home, our relationship was finished."

"And I never even knew he existed." Emma's voice sounded distant.

"I know. Afterward I couldn't help but wonder how we were able to live together for such a long time without discussing some of the most important issues in our lives. Instead, I was grateful that Elliot never asked any questions. Never put any explicit demands on me. And I asked very little about his background too, even if we did meet his sister occasionally. But, above all, I had no idea about his dreams. How he imagined his—well, our—future. And you can't live like that. Not in the long term."

"Many live like that, Maria. Without ever having to confront each other's hopes and dreams. It's sad and strange, but many do."

"What I wanted to try to make you understand is that I never secretly dreamed of having a relationship with a woman. That this was the reason for my earlier relationships being short-lived and superficial. No, I don't think I had ever even considered it. I don't think I consciously thought much about my private life at all. Of course, I met someone now and then. When you are single, you get introduced to other singles by well-meaning friends. But nothing serious came out of any date after Elliot. Not until I met Maya. I am not sure if you will believe me when I tell you that I actually never really thought about the fact that I was in love with a woman. Or that I hesitated even for a second for that reason. I simply thought of her as someone I loved. So the fact that she didn't come with me to the funeral had nothing to do with me not wanting to show up with a woman. That I was in the least uncomfortable. I wasn't. You see, to me, being with Maya was absolutely natural and absolutely perfect. I loved everything she was. What she looked like. Her perfume. Her voice. Her hands. The way she moved. Her laughter. Her thoughts and ideas. Because all of it together made her Maya. They were all expressions of who she was. And because it was so simple and natural to me, I thought it would be to others too. Of course it wasn't, but I chose never to take on board any negative comments or reactions. I loved Maya and nothing could change that. Watching myself here and now, I can't possibly imagine that anybody could ever enter my life in that way again. Man or woman."

"I listen to you telling me this, and I wish even more that I could have met her and spent time with you when you were the person your love made you. When I think about myself too. And I realize that I will never experience anything like that kind of love. When Olof left me, it wasn't the kind of devastating grief you carry. Actually, I wonder if it was grief at all. I think it might have been fear more than anything. I was scared. So terribly scared of having to live on my own. As you know, I have never done that. Not until now. And it is utterly frightening."

We sat opposite each other, in silence. I felt tired. But I didn't want to make a move. It felt like the dark room with the sea as a distant backdrop was the perfect setting for us.

"Have you opened the envelope?"

I shook my head.

"Are you going to?"

"I don't know. I haven't thought about it."

Actually, this was true. I hadn't given the envelope a thought. I had dropped it into the box by my bed. I realized now that this wasn't really the right place for it. The envelope didn't belong with the things I wanted to keep close to me. I didn't want it at all. I decided to put it somewhere else later. Or throw it away.

"There is nothing more I want know about Mother. Nothing I want."

Emma's eyes glittered in the flickering light from the small candles on the table between us. "Do you never wonder about her life? Her childhood?"

"Why should I? She was an adult when I met her. My mother. I was the child. She wasn't."

"But we are affected by our childhood, aren't we? Surely you and I are products of ours. And the older you get, the more clearly you can see the child in other people, I think. It's as if they're walking about looking like adults, still carrying inside the child they once were."

"We talked about that before. But I think you exaggerate the importance. I have met people who had awful childhoods yet grew up to become decent, considerate, and mature human beings. And the other way around."

"I still think it stays there, inside us. The little child we once were. Our memories. Our disappointments. But also all the good things. And perhaps we can pick and choose a little and decide what we want to hang on to."

"You're philosophical, aren't you? And I am sure you are a better person than I am. In every way. But we all do the best we can."

I met her eyes.

"But if it makes you happy, I will open the envelope. And absorb what's inside. I promise."

"It's not for my sake that you should do it. It's for yours, Maria. Only yours. And it's entirely up to you."

She stood up, a little unsteadily. Due to the long day or the wine, I couldn't tell.

"It was a really nice walk today. But now I can feel it in my entire body. So I'll retire. We're in for a full day tomorrow too. And a lunch to pack before we leave. Good night, Maria. And thank you."

I stayed in the silence. I couldn't imagine what the following day would be like. In the past we had often sailed with Pau in his little boat. Long, lazy days when the tourists in town became too much. Anchoring up in a cove somewhere. Swimming, playing music, reading.

Often, we brought friends and anchored side by side so we could jump between the boats. During the past year, I had not sailed. I wasn't sure if Pau still sailed as before, but I didn't think so.

I rose and turned on the computer.

To my surprise there was an e-mail from Anna.

Hi Maria,

I was happy to hear that mom is with you. Take good care of her. She needs you. And who knows, you might need her too?

Love,

Anna

I had no idea how to interpret this. Here they were, worrying about each other, I thought. Neither of them needs me. More likely, they need each other. So why couldn't they just look after each other without involving me?

What was wrong with us? What had created this hopeless inability to communicate frankly and clearly?

I opened the folder with my diary and wrote a few lines.

Everything feels different. I'm not sure if it feels better. Just different. Two days to go. I thought I would welcome her departure. Having my house

back. But now I'm not so sure. It's not that I want
her to stay. I don't think I do. I just don't want to
be alone here in the house again.

I suddenly felt exhausted. I took the sheets from the
basket where I kept them during the day, moved the
cushions from the sofa, and made my bed. I sat down and
picked up the box from the floor. I ran my palm over the
lid. It was a small one, about the size of a shoe box. I kept
my clothes and other things in one of the downstairs bedrooms. But what was in this box I wanted close by. Often
when I lay sleepless, I would open it and take out some
small item.

I carefully collected the photos that were still spread
out on the table and placed them in a small pile. I took out
the envelope and set it to one side. Underneath, there were
Maya's early letters. Her perfume bottle, almost empty,
but still carrying her fragrance. And there was my old
phone. I picked it up and stuck the charger in the wall
socket. I kept the phone charged so I could turn it on when
I needed to. Because inside there was Maya's voice. A few
voice messages she had left for me. And the pictures. A few
selfies of us on the terrace. A picture where Maya was
standing behind me, gathering my hair behind my ears.
One picture of us in profile, so close that our noses almost
touched. I flicked through them, as cautious as always.

Scared that some careless push of a key would erase them all. I left the phone charging but returned the pile of photographs to the box. The envelope sat on the table. I picked it up and held it in my hand for moment, hesitating. It did not belong in the box. In the end, I closed the box and put the envelope on top.

DAY FIVE

Pau was right about the weather. We couldn't have wished for a better day. I stood on the terrace, looking out over the sea as I did every morning. The sky was blue and without a cloud, and it looked like a light breeze rippled the glittering surface of the sea. There was not a person in sight. But Cadaqués always woke late, especially this time of year.

When I came downstairs, Emma was already busy packing our lunch, and there was little left for me to do.

"I hope this will be okay. It's really just some bread, cheese, and fruit."

"That's a lot, Emma. It looks perfect. It will be awkward if we bring too much."

"I'm not sure this is such a good idea," I said as I sat down.

"No, it feels a bit odd to me too. I'm not really used to the sea. As you know, I really don't like being on the water or in it. Plus I get seasick very easily. But the weather couldn't be better, so I'm hoping it will all turn out fine."

"I wasn't really thinking about that."

"No, I understand, I think. But perhaps you don't need to think further than today. This outing. Just be here and now for little while."

Here and now? But I didn't want to be here and now. I had no wish to sit in a sailboat with Emma and Pau all day. The idea made me cold with apprehension. And the familiar irritation made itself felt again.

"It might have been better if Pau had just taken you on this trip," I said, fully aware that I was distancing myself from Emma. The small steps we had taken to get closer to each other these past days suddenly felt unreal. And meaningless. "I have sailed here before."

"I'm here to spend time with you, Maria. I would never have accepted the invitation if you hadn't come along. I don't even know Pau."

I finished my coffee and stood up.

"All right. I guess we are ready, then. Shall we go and see if Pau is too?"

⚜

Pau's little sailboat was a classic single-masted Catalan fishing boat. Or I assumed it was. There were many similar ones in the harbor. It was a wooden boat, its exterior painted warm red and the interior pale yellow. The fitting had probably been adjusted when it stopped being used as a fishing boat, because now it had only three narrow thwarts and a small space for storage.

Emma accepted Pau's hand with grace as she stepped into the boat. She sat down and looked up at me with a thin smile.

"Push away as you jump on board," Pau said. As if it was the most natural thing in the world. As if I had done this many times before. I had been on many trips in this boat before, but it had always been Maya who did this part. I untied the rope and waited for Pau to give me a sign to jump on board. For a moment, I could see myself missing the step and ending up in the water. But when I finally pushed off from land and jumped, it felt simple and natural.

As soon as we left the bay and reached the open sea, the wind picked up and the sail stretched. It wasn't a strong wind, just enough to push us forward gently. I sat where I had landed, in the bow, and I leaned over the rail and looked down into the turquoise water.

Like Emma, I had avoided the sea all my adult life. I also avoided boats generally, and I didn't like swimming. My love of the sea was limited to observing it from land. And smelling it. Particularly here where it was associated with so many memories. The salty smell of the sea blending with Maya's perfume. Her voice with the constant backdrop of the sound of the sea. And then the music that was also forever connected with the sea. Lluís Llach especially. *"Bressol de tots els blaus,"* the cradle of all blue. The song Pau used to sing. In another life. It was all still there, inside me. Protected and indestructible. But I could experience it only from the outside. I could remember everything, but I couldn't re-create the mood.

I stretched further over the rail and let my hand breach the surface of the water, sending spray into the air. The sea was cool but not cold, and I lowered my head and felt the tiny droplets on my skin.

When I turned around and sat back, I realized that Emma had laid down on one of the thwarts, and she didn't look in the least uncomfortable. Her bare feet rested on the rail, and she was laughing at something Pau had said.

As I'd expected, we sailed north, past Cap de Creus and farther along the coast. The wind was still light, and we cruised leisurely in silence. Even though our pace was not fast, it was difficult to carry on a conversation across the boat and with the mast between us. This suited me just fine. I reclined and allowed the gentle October sun to warm my skin.

Pau took in the sail, and we anchored in a narrow cove. Two rocky islets protected the inlet. The rough volcanic rock that rose out of the sea looked like something covered in elephant hide, like parts of some gigantic body resting under the water.

Pau asked if we would like to go ashore, but we both shook our heads.

Pau and Emma talked. Mostly Pau, who had a lot to tell about the area, about the national reserve. He talked about the unusual geological conditions where the Pyrenees disappear into the Mediterranean. And about politics, of course. And Emma was an attentive listener. At least as far as I could tell. I picked up my book and began to read, but I struggled to focus. Now and then fragments of the conversation reached me, but I made no effort to participate. I watched the blue sky above and felt the boat gently rock below. This was how the other days had been. I thought of them as so many, but in reality it was really a couple of seasons. And not many trips each season.

"Did you bring your guitar?"

Pau seemed to startle and looked at me. He seemed to need a moment to collect himself.

"No. I don't play much these days."

We let it drop, and neither of us said anything further.

I had dozed off when I felt the boat rock as Pau stood up.

"What do you think? Are you hungry? Shall we make lunch?" We brought out the basket.

Then Pau took out his little grill.

"Oh, I was secretly hoping you had brought it!" I said, and I couldn't help smiling.

"Sardines?"

"Yes, only because they were bought fresh last night. I think Emma should get to taste them." He smiled as if our enthusiasm genuinely pleased him.

He placed the grill on the foredeck, and Emma and I spread a cloth over one of the thwarts and unpacked the food we had brought. Here it suddenly looked like a lot.

Bread, cheese, olives, tomatoes, peaches. I hadn't realized I was hungry. Now everything looked very tempting.

"Why don't you have a swim while I grill the sardines?" Pau said. He must have been thinking of Emma, that she really should take the opportunity to have a swim. He knew how I was with the sea.

Emma and I looked at each other in silence.

"The water is exceptionally clear here. It's a popular spot for divers."

When he didn't manage to get a response from us, he shrugged and focused on the grilling.

Emma seemed interested in what he was doing and asked questions about the fish.

Pau was squatting beside the grill, and Emma was on her knees, resting her elbows on the deck. In the stillness I could hear their voices but again I didn't make an effort to participate in the conversation. Instead, I turned and leaned over the rail again. The water was like glass, turquoise and so clear that I felt I could see all the way to the bottom.

The smell from the grill began to waft through the air.

Then we ate. The fish was the highlight, of course, but the things Emma had packed complemented it perfectly. The sun was warm; the water lapped against the sides of the boat. We sipped the white wine. I returned to the bow and lay down with my feet resting on the rail.

I heard Emma laugh again. A young, relaxed, and happy laughter. Almost sensual. As she must once have laughed a long time ago. She must have, but I had no memories of it. In my memory she was mute. I turned my head and looked at her. Now she sat across the thwart with one leg on either side of it. She was resting on her hands, which made her lean forward a little. She balanced her feet on the tips of her toes and her head was turned toward Pau, with her neck graciously bent backward. She was beautiful. A memory flashed past. For some reason, I was reminded of how I once watched her as she was lying asleep. I couldn't remember the circumstances, just the scene. Emma was little, a couple of years old perhaps. We were alone in the room. Perhaps she was having her nap. I leaned over her without really being aware of what I was doing or why. My face was so close I could feel her warm breath, but she was still asleep. Her blonde hair lay fanned out on the pillow, and I stretched out my hand and lifted a thin strand. I rubbed the soft hair between my fingers and smelled it. And when I moved my fingers to my nose, I could pick up her scent. It was light, barely perceptible, but it still surprised me. It made me think of flowers that only give off a fragrance when you crush their petals. Flowers that smell only when you destroy them.

The memory made me uneasy.

Emma sat as before, and I could hear fragments of their conversation. It came over me without a warning. An irresistible impulse.

I quickly stood up, pulled off my top, and stepped up onto the thwart. I didn't exactly dive in. I just took a step off the boat.

Then I sank. Deeper and deeper. I opened my eyes. The sun shot shafts of light through the turquoise water. I stretched out my hand and it cut through the light. All sounds were softened.

I sank.

I pressed my arms against my sides to reduce the resistance. But everything slowed down.

Eventually, I was suspended in the turquoise for a brief overwhelming eternity. My heartbeats passed through my skin and into the surrounding sea, which was infinite. Small particles drifted gracefully in the water where rays of sunshine continued to weave ribbons of lighter blue.

It crossed my mind that I could remain like that. I wanted it. But I began to rise slowly, relentlessly.

Then, suddenly, above me, a cloud of white bubbles. Vibrations against my skin. The notion that I was no longer alone. Something brushing against me. Rubbing against my leg.

I raised my arms over my head and I rose faster.

When I reached the surface, Pau stood leaning over the rail as if ready to jump into the water.

He took my hand and quickly pulled me on board.

Then he turned his head and searched the surface of the water.

"I don't know what happened. She just suddenly jumped in," was all he had the time to say before Emma's head broke through the surface and Pau again stretched out a hand.

Emma was gasping, and she seemed to struggle to stay afloat. But she didn't take Pau's hand. Without another thought, I jumped back in.

She fended off my hands when I stretched to embrace her. Instead, she kept flailing her arms and gasping for air. I took a couple of strokes and put my arms around her from behind.

"I'm holding you, Emma."

She kicked with her legs and waved her arms.

"I'm holding you."

I held her with one arm and took a few strokes toward the boat. Pau stretched down his hands, and with my help, he got a strong grip on Emma's arms and pulled her on board. It looked like he carried her whole weight, with no help from her. I saw that she scraped her leg against the rail before finally landing on board. When Paul had helped me up again, I sank down opposite Emma. She looked cold, and her white T-shirt hung wet and heavy on her body. Blood mixed with water ran from the abrasion on her leg.

"Here, take my top."

I held out my dry T-shirt, but Emma shook her head. She crossed her arms over her chest and avoided my eyes.

So I pulled on the top. Pau had found a beach towel in his bag and placed it over Emma's shoulders. She pulled it tight and nodded a thank-you.

Pau reached into his bag again.

"Here, have a little brandy. It will warm you up," he said, and placed three small glasses beside me on the thwart. We drank, but none of us said anything for quite a while. The alcohol burned all the way down.

"What is it with you two? Couldn't you let me know before you decide to take a swim?" Pau shook his head and walked over and sat down in the bow.

None of us said anything.

I shivered and realized it had gotten colder and the wind had picked up. The sky had turned a pale, icy blue. It was as if the wind had removed a layer that softened the blue before. When I threw Pau a glance, I realized he had noticed it too.

"Here, Emma, I have an extra pair of trousers in my bag. You look really cold . . ." I hadn't finished when she clumsily stood up in front of me.

"I told you I don't need anything!" She spoke quietly, and it was only her expression that showed how upset she really was. "Keep your damned clothes." Now it was a whisper. She had her back to Pau, and she was speaking Swedish, so I hoped he didn't get what she was saying. "Keep your damned Cadaqués. Your house. Which isn't even yours. You keep it all! I was an idiot to come."

The towel slid off her shoulders when she made a gesture to indicate all she didn't want to be a part of. The T-shirt was plastered over her breasts. I averted my eyes.

She took a step back, faltered, and the boat rocked. I could see that she was silently weeping. Then she sat down with a thud.

I took a deep breath and looked at Pau. He had started to clean the grill and seemed unconcerned. He whistled softly and I took it as a sign that he was trying to break up the unpleasant atmosphere.

"We are cold, both of us, and I think it looks like the weather is changing. Perhaps we should turn back?"

"You're right. The wind is picking up. Let's hope it's only temporary. It should be too early for the *tramuntana* anyway. And we don't have far to sail."

Pau smiled, but there was a crease between his eyebrows. From concern over the weather, irritation, or disappointment at how the day had developed, or for some other reason, I couldn't tell.

❧

The wind rose further during the return trip, and we arrived chilled to the bone. I watched as Emma said good-bye to Pau before gingerly getting to the stern and balancing on the deck. I had pulled the boat as close to the quay as possible to make it easier for her, and she jumped ashore without a problem. But she avoided my outstretched hand and carried on without a word. I helped Pau get our things from the boat, and then we slowly made our way back home. The wind blew down from the mountains, and it was as if there was no shelter from it anywhere.

"I'm sorry it ended the way it did. It was never my intention. I just had an impulse to jump overboard. I had no idea Emma would follow me. She is afraid of water."

It was a moment before Pau answered.

"I think she was afraid for your sake more than anything."

To my frustration, I could feel a lump in my throat and my eyes filling with tears.

"I had no idea she would react like that."

Pau slowed down and looked at me with a thoughtful expression.

"And I couldn't for the life of me imagine that you were going to jump in. I have never seen you swim before."

I made no comment, and he said nothing further. When we reached his house, we stopped briefly.

"I was going to ask if you would like to come down to my house tonight. But things being as they are, perhaps we should leave it for tomorrow. That's Emma's last night here, isn't it?"

He stood in front of the blue door, his hands full. For the first time in a long time, we looked straight at each other.

"It's been a long time since you visited," he said eventually.

I nodded.

"Yes, it's been a long time. Everything is a long time ago now."

He bent and set down his bags. Then he grasped my upper arms gently and pulled me close and gave me a quick kiss on either cheek. I just let it happen, feeling a little awkward.

"Thank you for a lovely day. It's been a long time since we sailed too." He picked up his bags.

"I'm so sorry the day ended the way it did. It was entirely my fault."

"I had a wonderful day, Maria. A day out sailing is never a bad day for me. I should have done it sooner. We should have."

His green eyes were red rimmed. I couldn't tell if it was the day on the sea, the wind, or something else. There was so much I didn't understand about Pau. Well, about other people generally. Emma said I thought I knew what other people were thinking. But I looked at Pau and had absolutely no idea what he was thinking.

"Yes, we should have done it sooner. We should have stopped. And we should have said more than those trivial phrases when we met."

He stood absolutely still and looked so sad that I again felt that lump in my throat. But the moment passed.

"Talk to Emma and let me know about tomorrow evening." And with that we parted.

❧

I neither heard nor saw Emma when I stepped inside. But I could still sense that she was home. I moved quietly as I unpacked the lunch basket in the kitchen, and then I went downstairs to have a shower. I stood under the running water until I felt warm again.

I made a fire in the large open fireplace in the kitchen and sat down in front of it. It was painful to revisit the afternoon's incident, but I couldn't help doing it. We had only one more day together, and I had caused this mess. I had made Emma come here, with my stupid invitation, and now I had ruined her visit with one more idiotic impulse. I had told Pau that I hadn't foreseen Emma's reaction. But was that really true? As Maya used to say, it was often more important to sort out your own thoughts than to spend effort trying to understand what thoughts other people might harbor inside their heads. So there I was, trying to understand why I had behaved the way I had. And I couldn't for the life of me find an answer. The impulse had caught me unawares. Me more than Pau and Emma even, I thought. It felt as if the time between the process in my brain and my body's response had been virtually nonexistent. The complete lack of control frightened me.

After a while, I went upstairs and sat on the terrace. It was cold, but it felt as if the wind had died down. The sky was still absolutely clear. A cold sun sat low and would soon disappear behind the hills. I left the door half-open and went inside and sat down on the sofa and placed the box on my lap. I had promised Emma to open the envelope. Ridiculously, it felt as though I would compensate her for today in a small way if I finally explored its contents.

I don't know what I expected. Whatever it was, it certainly wasn't what landed on the table when I emptied the envelope.

Cards. Birthday cards. One for each year since my nineteenth birthday. The last one was dated three years ago, when I turned forty-five. The first twelve cards were identical. Beautiful double cards with a drawn flower motif on the cover. She must have bought a whole packet. The text inside was short and more or less the same in each card.

My dear Maria,

Warm congratulations on your nineteenth birthday!

We miss you here and we think about you, hoping that you are happy.

Mother

As they stood, the words weren't particularly personal, yet I could clearly hear her voice behind the flowing handwriting. This was the first and only thing she had ever written to me. I placed the cards in little piles, five cards in each. Five piles. And two in the last one. After the first twelve, the cards were of different sizes and styles. And gradually the handwriting became less flowing. In the very last card, it was hardly legible. But I had no trouble deciphering it.

My dear Maria,

My warm congratulations on your birthday. I think of you constantly, and I hope that your life has turned out as you had hoped. That you have been able to shape it to your satisfaction. Above all, I hope you have found someone to love. Someone who understands how to love you. That is what I wish for you on your birthday.

Your mother

By now I was crying, of course. What was happening to me? It was as if someone had opened a tap and my tears flowed time and again. It didn't matter now. I was alone with the cards in front of me.

I started again. Read one at a time, starting with the first one. The slight variations were almost imperceptible, but the odd word that had been crossed out caught my eye. She must have changed her mind and started again, and I couldn't help but wonder what she had originally had in mind. Now I noted that the text grew a word or two longer with every card. Did they also become more personal and more emotional? Or was that just something I tried to read into them?

The big mystery was why she had never posted them, of course. She always knew where I lived, even though she never made any kind of contact. And we had met on the few occasions when I came back to visit. A few Christmases at Emma and Olof's home. The odd Midsummer. Nothing had ever made me think she had been writing these cards every year on my birthday in May. Or that she would even have remembered the day. Or, for that matter—and this was even harder for me to envisage—that she would have been thinking about me.

Would it have changed anything if she had posted the cards? I couldn't help but think that the impact was much greater this way. If she had sent me that first card, I would probably just have thrown it away, and it wouldn't really have touched me at all. But with them spread out in front of me, all these birthdays, all these words, it was impossible not to be moved. I could no longer ask her what she had meant. Why had she not posted them yet saved them?

It struck me that perhaps she had intended for me to sit just like this. Desperately trying to understand what her intention had been. It wasn't what I wanted to believe. I wanted to be allowed to embrace the words. And the thoughts behind each word. I wanted to believe them.

I awkwardly rose from the floor. There were still no sounds from downstairs. I wondered if Emma was asleep, and I wasn't sure whether she wanted to be left alone. Should I just sneak out and have a meal by myself in town? Or should I try to make myself a meal at home? That would inevitably wake her.

I considered the alternatives while I collected the cards and stuck them back into the envelope. And then I returned the envelope to the box. For now. Only until I had decided what to do with it.

I heard Emma in the kitchen while I was on my way downstairs. She stood leaning against the counter, a glass of water in her hand.

"Did you sleep?"

She shook her head.

"No, I can't really sleep during the day. Like I said, I can still get some rest. But not today. And I wasn't really tired. Just cold. And embarrassed." She sipped the water.

"I'm so sorry, Emma."

She shrugged.

"It's not your fault. I apologize for my behavior. I just lost it when I watched you disappear into the water. And then not resurface. I just panicked."

She looked at me, and I couldn't quite read her expression. Or perhaps I could. I just didn't want to.

"I have no idea why I jumped overboard. It just happened. You know how I am overcome by these mad impulses and do the most embarrassing things. Which I then regret. So I'm the one who should apologize."

"Pau must have thought we were mad, both of us." A little smile touched her lips, so brief I hardly caught it.

"Perhaps. I'm not sure. But he still invited us to come down to his house tomorrow. What do you say?"

Emma crossed the room and sat down at the table. She was pale and still looked as if she was cold. I put a couple of new logs on the fire. But in spite of the fire the spacious room felt cool.

"It all feels a little awkward, all of it. I don't know. What do you think?"

I stood by the door to the little balcony off the dining area. The view offered a glimpse of the sea. The sun had disappeared and dusk had dampened the light as well as the wind, it seemed. I turned and looked at Emma.

"I think we should accept." As soon as I had said the words, I realized how much I wanted to sit in Pau's study and hear him sing. I couldn't remember when I had last wanted something this strongly.

"Let's do that, then," Emma said.

༈

We had finished our meal. Leftovers from lunch. It amazed me how Emma was able to create something from hardly any ingredients at all. For the first time, we had our meal in the dining room. The fire had finally warmed up the room, and I could see that Emma's cheeks had their color back. Yet she still looked exhausted.

"I'm so sorry about what I said in the boat. It had nothing to do with you. Nothing to do with your jumping into the water. I mean, of course you had the right to do that. That it turned into such an incident is entirely my fault."

I hesitated, not sure what to say. "I could have said something before jumping. But it just came over me, like I said. And I just stepped off the rail. I had no idea it would make you so upset. I had no thoughts at all. Not that I was aware of anyway. I saw you sitting there. So comfortable and relaxed, talking to Pau. Laughing. I saw it, and it looked so . . . well, so beautiful. So absolutely perfect."

Emma slowly shook her head. Then she looked up at me and her eyes were very clear. I felt as if she could see right through me. Read my mind.

"I want to talk about Amanda."

My heart began to pound. I rose and took away our dinner plates and put out small ones for the cheese.

"You don't need to say anything, Maria. Just listen."

"And if I don't want to?"

"Then I can't make you. But I beg you. Listen to me. I have carried this for so long. I don't think I can manage any longer."

Although she was actually pleading, she didn't have the expression I had seen so often and disliked so. No, now she just looked determined, I thought. As if she had prepared herself carefully.

"Do you remember how it began?"

"What?"

"That afternoon."

"Of course I do."

"Do you mind listening while I tell you how I remember it?"

I leaned back against the chair. Even though the room was warm now, the metal felt cold against my back.

"It was your idea." She threw me a quick glance before continuing. "But, then, almost all ideas were, so that doesn't really matter. You were always leading and Amanda followed. And I think you challenged her more and more. Perhaps to force her to choose between you and me."

What she said hung in the silence between us. I said nothing.

"I can understand that now. You were almost sixteen, and I had just turned ten. Of course you wanted to do your things. But Amanda always had to tug me along. There was nobody else. Mother was never there to reckon with. You know that. Always somewhere else. Even when she was at home. But you got impatient and tired of me. And Amanda was torn between us. It was like you found increasingly more challenging things for us to do. Things I couldn't really do. Or things I wasn't allowed to do. Like that day. When you decided that we were to go down to the canal. Thinking about it, I'm not sure if you actually said it. Or if you just started to walk."

She seemed to be considering what she had said.

"No, I don't think you told us to follow. I'm not sure if you said anything at all or if so, what it might have been. But you didn't really make the decision for us. No, I think you just casually said that *you* were going to the canal. As if to see what would happen. But to us it was the same thing. We followed you wherever you went. We all knew that it was absolutely forbidden."

The canal was forbidden territory at all times. The water was polluted by sewage so we were not allowed to swim there in the summer. But in the winter it was an absolute no-go zone. When the water had frozen over. Even when the ice was at its thickest, a channel was kept open for the regular boat traffic. And the water never froze at all where the sluice flowed into it. Our side of the canal faced north, and the ice thawed last along that shore. Just as the snow lasted well into spring under the dark pine trees on the slope down to the water. Not even during warm summer days did the sun reach there.

"I can't understand what made you go there that day."

I went to collect another bottle of wine from the fridge. When I held it out to top up Emma's glass, she quickly placed her hand over it and shook her head. I filled my own glass and sat down.

"It was so cold. Do you remember? The first week of March. Overcast, gray, and deserted. Hardly any snow remained and icy patches froze over during the night and thawed during the day. But that particular day it was colder and everything was frozen. The whole world was gray. The road was slippery, and I kept slipping and almost fell over a couple of times. So we lagged behind, Amanda and I. You were ahead of us, and you walked fast. And the distance between us kept growing. I think Amanda tried to keep your pace, but she was held back by me."

Emma bit her lip.

"I can see her so clearly, Maria. How she struggled. Torn between her yearning to walk beside you. Be near you. Talk to you. Be part of your adventures. Share your secrets. And her responsibility for me."

I closed my eyes. I didn't want to see Emma. And more than anything I didn't want to listen to her. But I stayed where I was, helpless, unable to say or do anything.

"So we came down to the canal. There was still snow under the trees on the slope down to the water. Grayish and with a hard, icy crust. It was completely still. That's how I remember it anyway. I could hear the sound of your boots when they broke the crust. Some crows cawed over the black treetops. But I remember it as silent otherwise. As if everything was holding its breath."

I opened my eyes and saw that Emma was standing. She walked to the balcony door and stood there with her back to me, looking out.

"Is it okay if I have a cigarette here?"

She turned her head and looked at me, and I nodded.

"Of course."

I held my glass in a tight grip. We needed our drugs, both of us. Emma lit a cigarette and blew the smoke through the open door.

"When Amanda and I reached the edge of the canal, you were already out on the ice. You said nothing. There was no need to. Like I said, you never had to lead us on. We followed wherever you went, and you never turned to see if we were there. And you didn't this time either. You just charged ahead, knowing full well that we would follow. And you jumped so easily over the cracks. Moved so fast and with such ease. Amanda held my hand, and we followed in your tracks. But so much more slowly. The distance kept increasing. When we got further out and closer to the open water, there were more cracks and they were wider. And the ice floes moved under our feet. Here and there you could see water well forth between the cracks. I don't remember that we said anything, but I thought I could feel Amanda's fright through her hand that held mine in a hard grip. And I became scared too. Then she stopped. We stood still and I heard her panting. Then she called out to you. Called to say that we wanted to turn back. But you made no sign of having heard her. We stood there for a while. I'm not sure I'm right, but it felt as if Amanda was hesitating. That scared me too, because she used to be so sure of what to do. You were just a dark figure in the gray-white landscape, far ahead of us. Then we could see that you changed direction and turned back toward the shore. But you didn't come toward us. You moved in a wide curve and seemed to aim for the shore much farther away. Again, you moved gracefully, running fast and skipping over the cracks. So we turned too and moved in your direction, aiming for the same stretch of shore. We walked over untouched ice, instead of following our own tracks back to the shore. We no longer held hands. I think Amanda was relieved. She walked ahead of me, and I could tell from her posture that she was her usual self again. She talked about what we were going to do when we got home. She was going to make us hot chocolate. I watched her jump over a wide crack and land on the other side of it. There she turned to check that I got over safely. But just at that moment, the crack widened further and the ice creaked under our feet. I saw water gushing up over the ice on both sides. Amanda took a step back as if to avoid the water."

I could hear that Emma was crying.

"I felt ice cold water wash over my boots. And I watched how Amanda suddenly tottered and slipped before she slid into the dark water between us. It was strange how slowly it seemed to happen. So quickly yet so unbearably slowly. I can't remember any sounds at all. No screams for help. Not even any sounds of splashing water. Nothing. It was as if the water had swallowed Amanda in no time at all and absolutely silently. One moment she was standing there, talking about hot chocolate. The next moment she had disappeared, and the ice creaked as the floes drifted apart. She never resurfaced. I stood there, completely speechless, as if waiting for it to rewind. A miracle. For something that could undo what had happened. My teeth began to chatter. A ship passed through the channel in the ice, farther out, and the swell reached me and I felt its movement under the ice. Then I must have turned and started to walk back to the shore. I must have, but I have no memory of doing it. I must have followed our tracks back toward land, the way we had come. I slipped and I stumbled and finally I began to cry. When I came closer to the shore, a man came walking his dog. A golden retriever. When he asked what was the matter, I couldn't speak at first. I wasn't able describe what I couldn't understand. But he crouched down in front of me, looked at me, and gazed out over the ice. He pulled me close for a moment. He told me to wait and ran out on the ice, following our tracks. But there was nothing out there for him to see. Nothing. Somehow I think he understood what must have happened. He turned back and came running toward me, he too slipping on the ice. He looked around as if hoping to find some help. But there were just the two of us and the dog. By now my crying was unstoppable, almost choking me. He asked where I lived and took me by the hand. He talked all the way, as if trying to comfort me, but nothing he said made any sense to me. It was as if he wasn't really there. As if the man, the dog, well, the entire world, was very distant. And I was completely alone."

I opened my eyes and looked at Emma, who had turned toward me.

"But you, Maria, you never looked back. You just walked your way."

Emma stretched out her hand and put out the cigarette on the balcony rail, walked to the kitchen counter, where she wet the butt under the tap before dropping it in the waste bin. Then she returned to her chair and sat down. I had the distinct impression that she purposely took her time. She placed her hands on the table and clasped them. But she said nothing further.

"It wouldn't have made any difference if I had been there," I said eventually. "Nobody could have saved Amanda."

Emma's eyes were wide open, and she regarded me with a steady gaze.

"No, nobody could have saved Amanda. Not there, not then. But we would have come with you if you had only waited for us. We would have walked in another direction if you had only waited."

"It was an accident. And I never asked you to come in the first place. And I didn't choose the path you took over the ice."

"True. It was an accident. It could have happened to either of us. You or me. For a long time, I wished it had been me. I dreamed about how I slid down into the ice-cold darkness under the ice. Strangely, I never dreamed about watching Amanda doing it. It was always me."

She looked genuinely intrigued. As if the thought had never struck her before. She lowered her eyes and looked at her hands. She seemed to hesitate about whether to continue. He previous confidence seemed completely lost. Now she seemed to search for every word.

"It might not have made any difference for Amanda if you had been with us when it happened. You are right. Nobody could have saved her."

She wiped her mouth with her palm, placed her elbow on the table, and rested her cheek on her clenched hand. She was silent for so long that I wondered if she had finished. I made as if to stand up. Then she stretched her hand across the table, and I sank down on my chair again.

"But to me, it would have made a world of difference, Maria." She covered her face with her hands and sobbed.

I sat opposite her helplessly, unable to move. It took her a long time to collect herself.

"I had nobody to talk to. I had to describe how the accident had happened, of course. But I hardly understood it myself, so how could I describe it to others? But, Maria, there was one thing that scared me more than anything else afterward."

I felt my pulse pound and my cheeks flush. I couldn't find anything to say.

"Mother came toward us through the hallway when we got back. Then everything turned into chaos. The police arrived. Neighbors we didn't even know. The man with the dog stayed for a long time. I remember he sat with me on the sofa, holding me."

She looked straight at me.

"But you stood by the window all the time, Maria. I have always wondered what you were thinking. Why you never said a word to me. Never asked me anything. Never made any effort at all to comfort me."

The room went deadly silent, and the sound of voices from outside drifted in.

"You think people who lose someone they love should be able to unite in grief. Comfort each other, even. But there you were, by the window, with your back toward me. And Mother. She didn't cry. She didn't hold me. She didn't even run to call the police when we first arrived—the man with the dog did that. She just stood there. And I looked at her and realized she didn't even see me. She just looked scared. Not sad. Not shocked. Just bewildered. That's what it looked like. As if she had no idea what to do. And when we stood there at first, and you came out of your room. You must have heard, of course. You already knew. And you saw us. But you said nothing. Nothing at all. You just walked past us into the living room. And there you stood the entire time, in front of the window, turned away from us. I longed for you to hold me. For us to hold each other. I wanted you to help me make sense of the senseless. Later, when everybody had left and all was still, well, then you just left. You had not one word for me. Not one look. And I felt you were accusing me. As if it was my fault."

I slowly shook my head.

"That's not what I was thinking. Not at all, Emma. I just couldn't do anything other than what I did. I just had to leave."

Again the room became silent.

"But you left me behind, Maria. You left me with Mother. I had nobody to turn to. Nobody to tell me how to survive. What to do."

"Nobody helped me either. And that's how it is, more often than not, I think. Two people grieving the same loss are rarely able to help each other. Grief is private. You're alone in your grief."

"I knew you had no interest in me. But afterward, it was as if you couldn't even stand being in the same room with me. I have a memory from when I was really little. I'm not even sure if it is a memory. But I think it is. I couldn't have made it up. It's too strange. I think I had been having a nap, so I must have been very little. A couple of years old, perhaps. I was half-awake when I noticed that you came up to my bed and bent down over me. Although I was so little, I somehow understood that I shouldn't open my eyes. So I stayed still. I felt how close you were. I heard your breath by my ear. Then you did something really strange. I really do think I understood how extraordinary it was. I realized that you had never come this close to me ever before. But then you took a strand of my hair between your fingers. And I think you smelled it. It was just a brief moment. Then you disappeared out of the room. I have never understood what made you do that."

"I remember. Strange that you should mention it now. For some reason I thought about it earlier today. It's the only time I have ever been close enough to you to pick up your scent. Amanda's scent was like my own. I couldn't distinguish between the two. But your hair had your scent. I remember that."

That pleading expression was back on Emma's face. But I had nothing more to give her. I couldn't understand my own action. I had no memory of what preceded it. It was just an isolated scene without context.

"You never took the slightest interest in me. It was as if I was something Amanda carried around. Something you hoped she would put down."

I nodded. "But I realized that you were a real person. And sometimes when I saw you with Amanda, and you seemed to be having a good time together . . . or were just comfortable in each other's company . . . Well, then I just wanted to walk away."

"But why do you do that all the time? Why do you leave, Maria? Why don't you wait a little before you make up your mind? Give people some time to explain? Why do you think you know their innermost emotions? That you know what they think? Amanda loved you. You first. Me, she adopted, and I loved her for it. I loved her the way a child ought to love a mother. But I am not sure if Amanda really loved me. I needed her. I'm not sure I would have survived without her. Do you remember what it was like, Maria? How lonely we were? For me, Amanda was my mother. I loved her. I trusted her. And she never failed me. But I think I always knew that you came first. That it was really you and Amanda. And I think I knew already then how hard it was for Amanda to choose between the responsibility for me and her love for you. And you know, I don't think she ever chose me. She just realized that I wouldn't survive without her. That is a terrible responsibility for anyone. And Amanda was just a child. I think she hoped you would understand. But you turned your back on her, Maria! Like you have done with everybody else. You just walk away when not everything is to your satisfaction. But nothing is perfect! Sometimes you have to make do with what you can get. But you, you had to have everything! And you expected too much. From everybody. Didn't you understand how devastated Olof was when you left? Did you not consider him at all?"

"I just had to get away. I couldn't stand it any longer. And I couldn't let him know about the pregnancy. I just couldn't be with him anymore. It was a matter of survival for me."

"What was it you couldn't stand? What burden did you have that I didn't have too?"

"You? You were in the sunniest place! Beautiful, successful, and loved. Your father adored you. However disgusting I found him, I could see that he loved you. And to Mother, you were finally the daughter she had wished for. Amanda and I, we were a mistake. A tragic mistake. But you, you were proof that Mother had finally achieved success."

Emma shook her head.

"She never wanted me. It was my father. And the life he was going to provide for her. The life that only ever existed in Mother's imagination. And when it all toppled, when Father was exposed in his shabby degradation, when the money was lost and the love was over, well, there she was, left with me. I was a tangible reminder of her failure. And I knew that when she looked at me, she didn't see me at all. But when she talked about you, it was always with admiration. Your successes. And *your* father's love grew in her imagination till she had made him into something he never was. When she looked back on her life, it was never the life she had really lived. She reshaped it. All her life she stepped out of one life and into another one. She started afresh again and again. But I was there, a shackle around her ankle. A constant reminder and proof of the present reality as well as the past. So you see, Maria, I'm the one who got the crumbs when it comes to love. You were offered everything, but you didn't think it was enough. You never stayed long enough to give anything time to develop. You were never willing to wait for anything. And you were never able to share. It had to be yours and yours only."

What could I say? I looked at my sister and knew it was the truth. But it was her truth. Not mine.

"When Amanda wasn't there anymore, it got absolutely empty. The whole world died." I searched for words, hunted in a void.

"I couldn't see. I heard nothing. I desired nothing. It was as if I had died too. I truly felt like I was dead. How could I ever have been able to offer you anything?"

I paused.

"You say that it was in my power to change everything. But I had no power whatsoever. It's not possible to foresee an accident. Do you really think I would have gone out on the ice that day if I had known how it would end? You seem to think everything I do is calculated. That I have some intention in everything I do. But I'm just like anybody else.

Usually, I have no intention at all. Nowadays, I never do. I put one foot ahead of the other without thinking about where I'm headed. And that's how it was that day too. I never asked Amanda to come along. I'm not sure I knew where I was going. But it was such a gray, hopeless day. We were alone at home, as usual. And I just couldn't stand it. So I went out.

"And then I found myself by the canal. And then I just continued. I had no plan. Not for myself, and certainly not for you and Amanda. But when I heard Amanda call out, I knew she was scared. So I turned back toward the shore. I assumed you did the same. That we were heading back, all three of us. Just as when we came, I walked ahead, toward home, not looking back. Leaving you to do what you wanted."

I listened to my own voice with the same concentration as I had listened to Emma's. Our stories lay side by side for the first time. I had come to understand Emma's terrible grief, of course. Perhaps her sense of guilt too. I had understood them intellectually. But I had never before *felt* them. Never hers. Always only my own. Now, for the first time, I could see her on that wobbling ice floe. So little and so alone. Panic stricken and in shock. And for the first time, I could see myself reach the shore and climb the snowy slope with not so much as a look over my shoulder. Why had I not turned around? Checked if they were following? It wouldn't have changed the inevitable. But it would have changed how things evolved later on. It might have made both Emma and me different people. It might even have changed our lives. Instead, I just walked away.

It was true what Emma had said: I couldn't stand looking at her afterward. She was a constant reminder of what had happened. I don't think I ever put any blame on her. Not consciously. Just on myself. But to see her was to stick a pin into my heart. The pain of remembering was unbearable. I just couldn't take it. I walked on glass, and even the slightest reminder of my enormous guilt could cause everything to collapse. Emma's silent plea for my attention was intolerable. I had absolutely nothing to give her. In my desperation I might even emotionally have blamed her, in spite of knowing this was wrong. The little ten-year-old couldn't have done anything to prevent the accident. I knew Amanda had led the way and chosen the direction. But I needed somewhere to place the blame, and I placed it on Emma. Anywhere, just not on myself.

I looked at Emma's pale face and I could see that the blame had been there all the time, irrespective of me. That she had carried it all her life. Just like I had carried mine. I saw now that it had been in my power to relieve her of it. That I could have set her free. I had been able to do it then. I might even be able to do it now.

But I had no idea how. How to release both Emma and myself from what we had carried for so long, from something that had come to be a part of ourselves. I just couldn't imagine how this monumental liberation could be done.

Emma stood up.

"I know it wasn't your fault. It wasn't mine either. But as with much of what we experience in life, we are not just shaped by the incidents themselves. How we react to them is at least as important. How we deal with them afterward. There was nothing either of us could have done about the accident. But afterward, there were choices. And there have been choices ever since. I could have talked to you earlier. I could have visited you a long time ago. Written to you. Tried to forgive you. And myself. But I did nothing. I mourn the person I could have been all these years had I just made an effort. Instead, over time, I think I began to like that hopeless sense of guilt. Somehow it merged with my love of Amanda. I carried it and gradually it came to define me."

I was standing too. Awkwardly we stood facing each other with the table between us, both of us holding on to the backs of our chairs. As if we needed support. Or perhaps a protective shield.

"I am grateful, Maria. Not just for you having me here. But for what you have told me. And even more for having listened to me. I don't think you understand how apprehensive I was. And how relieved I am now. Now there is only one day left. It will be a very different day. A hopeful day, I think. I hope."

When she passed me on her way to her room, her hand touched my arm softly. I said nothing and I didn't move.

I heard her door close, and I was alone in the room.

I cleared the table and went upstairs and sat down on the terrace.

It occurred to me that the greatest, most formative experiences in our lives seldom become active memories. Instead, it is as if they spread in our bodies. They are pumped around by our hearts, circulating until they have left impressions in all our cells. That is how it was with me and Amanda's death. I knew what had happened, of course. I remembered it in a theoretical sense. If someone had asked me how my sister died, I would have been able to give a correct answer. But during all these years I had not considered the details, just lived with the insufferable regret. With the darkness and the emptiness. But now I couldn't escape Emma's words. I saw her as she was that day, the little ten-year-old girl. She appeared in her red jacket and the blonde fringe visible beneath the brim of her hat. A little snotty and very pale. And I saw how relieved Amanda was when she started toward the shore. A little disappointed too, perhaps, or annoyed because I had chosen another way back. I saw her turn now and then, making sure Emma was following, perhaps a little uneasy still. I heard her talk eagerly about what they were going to do when they got back home, about the hot chocolate she was going to make. I thought I could see how they calmed and comforted each other. I saw the whole course of events evolve. From the moment I decided to leave and put on my jacket, hat, and mittens. How I left the stuffy apartment where everything stood still. I felt, rather than saw, how Amanda and Emma hurriedly dressed too. I saw myself walk ahead of them. Without looking at them. Without thinking. What was I feeling?

I was angry.

I was jealous.

I could see that clearly now. But why I went for the canal, I still couldn't understand. Not even now, when I was really trying to remember. Perhaps I was hoping Amanda would stop me. That she would remind me we weren't allowed down there. Force me to stop and look at her. That I would somehow be able to make her promise some time for just the two of us, later. If I turned and followed her back home. But she said nothing at all. Not to me. I could hear her talking to Emma. But I couldn't hear what she was saying. It wasn't much. I realized they were struggling to keep up with me, and perhaps I purposely walked faster. Perhaps again I hoped to be stopped. That Amanda would ask me to slow down, wait for them. But she didn't. She never once called out to me. I don't think I had a plan. One thing just led to the next. Suddenly I was walking through the hard snow on the slope leading down to the canal. And then I was out on the ice. It surprised me a little. But I was more filled with a sense of excitement. It was chilling to see the black water between the cracks in the ice. Watch it well up as the weight of my body moved the ice floes and made them wobble.

I could feel tears slowly trickling down my face. These last few days had brought such a profusion of tears. More tears than I had shed during my entire life before.

I wasn't scared out there on the ice. I realized that it was dangerous, but it didn't really scare me. Instead, I was just excited. I wasn't thinking. I half-ran over the uneven ice and jumped from floe to floe. When Amanda called out, I must have heard. I must have, because that was when I turned back toward the shore. Not to where Amanda and Emma were but farther along, over untouched ice.

It hurt. And the pain was getting worse. As if I was approaching something I had been desperately avoiding. Something I didn't want to remember. When I heard Amanda call to me, I realized she was afraid. But not for herself, for Emma. That's what I thought. And it made me furious. Without Emma, we would have shared the excitement. Jumped across the cracks together. Chased each other over the ice. We would have shared the adventure. The chilling dangers. And if a crack had widened before us, it would have swallowed both of us. Together.

But now I had heard Emma's story. And now I realized that Amanda might have been afraid for her own sake too.

Not just for Emma's. That she would never have run with me over the ice, even if it had only been the two of us. If I had just stopped in my tracks and turned back to join them, she would have waited. And we would have walked back together in our tracks.

We would have shared that experience instead.

DAY SIX

We had established a kind of morning routine. Again I found Emma at the table on the patio when I came downstairs. And again she had bought croissants. There was a smell of coffee and cigarettes. It surprised me how right it felt. And how much I enjoyed it.

I poured my coffee and sat down.

"The last day. Anything in particular that you would like to do?"

Emma shook her head. "I'm happy just to take a stroll in town. Don't feel that you have to take care of me. That you need to fill my day."

I looked at her. She had a light tan by now and it suited her.

"It's a shame we don't have more time. There is so much I would like to show you. We could have gone to Barcelona, and I could have taken you to see Maya's gallery, which is really mine, even though it's hard for me to understand. I would have liked to hear your impression. I need some advice. I have put off making decisions ever since Maya died. But now I think the day when I have to return to real life is fast approaching. I have to decide what to do. Return to my school. Or trust that I will be able to make a living from the gallery."

"I suppose it's the same for me. I will go back home to face my difficult decisions."

In the ensuing silence, I could hear the little red-breasted bird in the fig tree. I got up and swept the crumbs from my croissant into my hand and placed them on the wall. Almost instantly the bird appeared and picked them up.

"Imagine how worried I was at the thought of having you here in the house."

Emma smiled. "Me too. I wondered how it would work. If I was intruding. But this might be just right. We can allow this to sink in. And see what to do in the future."

"You know, Emma, I really think we should go back to Port Lligat today. Have lunch at that little fish restaurant."

Emma agreed, but first she wanted to walk down to the town. She wanted to buy some small presents for Anna and Jakob.

✤

A kind of peace settles over Cadaqués when summer is over. People do ordinary things. Many bars, boutiques, and restaurants close, and those that remain open somehow seem changed, as if staff and customer are family. It might be true, I suppose. People move at a different pace, neither slowly like tourists nor fast like rushed shop assistants and waiters. It's as if the whole place exhales and returns to its normal life. The past summer was the first I had experienced in the house. It might also be the last.

Emma had spotted a pair of earrings in a store near the cathedral, and we strolled in that direction.

"I can't quite remember now how I envisioned your life here. But not quite like this."

"In what sense?"

"Well, I did think of you in a place by the sea. I told you, didn't I? And I knew it would be a beautiful place. But I still didn't think of it like this. Not this . . . well, this homey. This peaceful and . . . kind."

I laughed.

"If you had come here in July or August, I don't think you would have found it peaceful. And I don't think you would have described it as homey. Certainly that is not a good description of my house. Not the way I keep it."

"I didn't mean just the fact that the tourist season is over. It's the place itself. And perhaps even more you."

"Me?"

"Yes. During all these years when we have only seen each other sporadically, I have tried to imagine what your life would be like. Even if I knew where you lived, I never saw you in your environment. Just at my place on a few occasions. So I tried to paint a picture in my mind. I tried to envision it. What you did, how you lived. What people you socialized with."

"I never imagined you were thinking of me. Or that you would try to picture my life. On the other hand, I must admit that, arrogantly, I thought I knew everything about yours. Based only on my impressions from those dinners at your place. Christmas Eves and birthdays. Not a good basis, I'm sure. I realize that now. But all those years, I thought that was enough for me to understand what your life was like. But I knew nothing, did I?"

"Well, you don't know anything about other people, even if you live near them. I now look at Olof and he is a stranger. I have no idea what he might be thinking. What his dreams are. But during all those years, I did think I knew. I created an Olof for me who, I can see now, had very little likeness to the person he is."

We arrived at the shop and went inside. Emma pointed out the earrings she wanted to buy for Anna. I could see how well she had chosen. They were simple, just a beaten silver plate and a few rough pieces of red coral.

"What do you think, Maria?"

"They are perfect." I stressed the words to make sure she understood that I thought she had chosen well. "Absolutely perfect."

"There's not much I feel confident buying for her. Never clothes, for example. I am so unsure of what she likes. But when I saw these, I thought she might like them."

She asked to have them gift wrapped, and we walked down to the harbor and had a cup of coffee.

"It will be harder to choose something for Jakob."

"Tell me a little about him. I feel as if I don't know him at all. Not like Anna. I have only met him on a few occasions over the years. And we have never really gotten to know each other."

"No, I know. It's not easy to get close to him. Like I said earlier, he was very shy as a small child. Afraid of strangers. Perhaps it was my fault. I think I kept him too close to me. I didn't really let go of him. With Anna, it might have been the other way around. Perhaps I pushed her away."

Emma sat with her elbows rested on the table and her hands covering her mouth. I was afraid she would start to cry again, so I made sure not to comment on what she had said.

"I don't think I ever considered having children. When I became pregnant, I never thought of it as a child. It was inconceivable that Olof and I were to have a child. I just couldn't accept it. But I do think Olof was made to be a father. It was me. There was something wrong with me. Perhaps I never knew how to be a mother. We didn't have much of a role model, did we?"

Emma lowered her hands and looked at me.

"This is so sad, Maria. Because I really do think that you would have been a good mother. But as for me, I think perhaps I really needed to grow up first. I should have learned how to live. When I had Anna, I experienced none of what other mothers describe. The normal reactions. How they instinctually know how to relate to their baby. How they give their baby their breast and feel invincible. I looked at my little baby and felt nothing. Nothing at all. Possibly a slight unease. Insecurity. It was as if I nursed her according to a manual. Nothing felt in the least bit natural. I wasn't able to breastfeed her. I took her to the clinic and had her weighed once a week to make sure I fed her enough. I couldn't judge if I put too many clothes on her or not enough. I remember how this enormous task that felt so utterly unnatural drained me completely. With Jakob, it was very different."

"When Anna came and spent time with me that summer, I thought she was an extraordinary little creature. I think it might possibly be the only time in my life when I have felt a longing for a child. And I envied you having her. It might not have been a conscious feeling, but now I realize it's probably true. But it wasn't a longing to give birth. I just became attached to your child. The human being she was. I don't think you should reproach yourself for things you think you did wrong. Just love her."

Emma didn't answer, but she nodded slowly.

"Do you know why I asked you to take Anna that summer?"

I shook my head.

"You never asked, and I was so relieved. I think it was the first time I was able to acknowledge, even to myself, that I was depressed. I could hardly make myself get out of bed. Dress. Everything seemed very distant. Even the sounds felt deadened. The colors faded. I lost all sense of time. I could sit on a chair in the kitchen for hours. I think Olof knew what was wrong with me. But somehow he also drifted out of focus. I no longer saw him."

Her eyes were on my face, but I wasn't sure if she really saw me.

"But what scared me the most was that I no longer saw the children. Anna was out a lot. She had lots of friends and managed on her own. But for Jakob, who was with me all the time, it must have been so frightening when I didn't take any notice of him. So Olof took Jakob and went to his parents' summer place. I'm not sure what he was thinking when he left Anna with me. Perhaps he left the responsibility with her. She was always so capable.

"But this was wrong. I think I realized that, somehow. And it scared me. I was scared of what I might do. What might happen. Scared of how it would affect Anna, watching me fall ever deeper. I was ashamed too. So I didn't want to involve anybody else. When I heard you were coming to Sweden for the summer holidays, I called you. And you said yes. Just like that. No questions. You have no idea how grateful I was. It was like a heavy burden had been lifted from my shoulders. And I survived, didn't I? We all did. And everything returned to some kind of normal existence. For some time. I had relapses, but never as bad as that summer. Still, I have never been able to let go of the thought that my illness has affected my children."

"I don't know them, so I can't give you an answer. Besides, it's an impossible question. The eternal one. Who we would have become given other circumstances. I am sure you have given your children so much more than your illness. I know that you love them. I'm sure they know that too. And that is enough. It is only when there is no love that there is no hope."

"I think I loved Jakob too much. And with time it was as if he was the adult and I was the child. Because it was I who needed him, not the other way around. I needed someone who needed only me. I never let him go. But now he lives with Olof, and I think it is good for Jakob. Good for both of them."

"What is Jakob interested in?"

"Music, first. I don't know if I already told you, but he studies at the Royal Swedish Academy of Music in Stockholm.

It may not lead to a job he can live off, but it is all he has ever wanted to do. He plays several instruments, but his real interest is composing. Writing music. He has always done that, ever since he was small. I tell myself it will work out for him. Olof has always struggled to accept the children's choices. He has accepted it now, but I think that deep down he is disappointed. I think he had in mind for them both to have an academic career. But Anna never hesitated. She knew exactly what she wanted to do. And Olof never tried to put pressure on her. It's not possible with her. Never was. She follows her own path. And in a way it is the same with Jakob. Even though he appears shy and cautious, he doesn't budge once he has made up his mind."

"It would be nice to see him. My nephew."

Emma smiled. "I'm sure that can be arranged."

"So, shall we look for something to do with music for him?"

We found nothing that Emma felt was right. After wandering around for quite a while, she finally decided on a ceramic salad bowl. I looked at her, surprised.

"He loves to cook too," she said. When I wondered if it wouldn't be difficult to bring with her, she just said "It will be worth it."

In the early afternoon, we walked to Port Lligat as we had decided. It was windy but the sun shone from a clear sky. On the way down the hill, Emma stopped several times to take in the view. It looked as if she was trying to memorize it.

The small restaurant was half-empty, and Marcello was as welcoming as always. When he heard that it was the last day of Emma's visit, he insisted on treating us to a glass of cava before our meal.

We raised our glasses and toasted.

"Come back, Emma."

I think we were both equally surprised.

"Oh, you will regret those words, Maria," Emma said, laughing.

"Yes, probably," I said.

We returned home slightly affected by the wine, the wind, and the sun, and Emma retired to her room. I sat on the terrace, as usual. We certainly had our routines by now. But I seemed to have lost some of my previous habits. I hadn't written a word in my diary for a few days, for example. Normally, I wrote every day. Often extensively. But since Emma's arrival it had only been a few short lines. Realizing this, I went inside and turned on the laptop.

I checked my mail and noticed there was one from Elna at the gallery. Without explaining why, she asked if we could make a time to meet the following week. As far as I knew we had nothing in particular to discuss. The plans for the spring were in place. I couldn't help but think she was making contact now, toward the end of the year, in order to pull me back to the gallery in a gradual, natural way. I replied that I would be happy to meet and suggested a time.

Emma leaves tomorrow. My feelings surprise me. I never wanted her here. Now I don't want her to leave. Not yet. My house smells of coffee in the morning and food at night. I can feel someone breathe here. Next week I'll go to Barcelona. Life intrudes from different directions. And I'm no longer resisting. I think.

Emma stood by the balcony door in the dining room. She wore a sleeveless white dress and light silver sandals. From behind, she looked like a young girl. Suddenly I felt very old. I had been looking forward to the evening at Pau's, but the warm anticipation dissolved and I felt tired.

Emma turned around when she heard me. She looked at me, her head a little cocked. Although she said nothing, I could tell from her expression that she thought I could have made more of an effort. I had just thrown on what I was used to wearing: jeans and a T-shirt. Both clean. But that was really all you could say about them.

I shrugged.

"You look nice," I said. It wasn't really a compliment but a comment filled with mixed emotions. I couldn't tell how Emma took it.

"Why don't you dress up a little too, Maria?"

"Why? This is fine."

"Oh, because it's my last evening here perhaps. Or just for your own sake. Because it makes you feel good to look good sometimes. Or just for whatever reason. Or no reason at all."

We faced each other and neither of us said anything. Suddenly I felt ridiculous. Like an obstinate child.

"Shall we go and take a look in your wardrobe? See what you have?"

I allowed myself to be pushed downstairs, and Emma threw open the door to my wardrobe. Not a very encouraging sight, exactly. She went through the few garments and finally she took out my red dress.

"Not that one," I said, trying to take it from her.

"Why not? This color suits you."

"Not that one!" I said. I tore the dress from her hand.

Emma looked astonished. And again I felt ridiculous. And teary eyed.

"Stop it! I told you I don't want to do this. Let's leave."

I managed to say the words and to hang the dress in the wardrobe. It took me a moment to pull myself together, and then I turned.

Emma had dropped her dress to the floor. It lay by her

feet, and she stood in front of me wearing just her panties and bra. Then she unhooked the bra and took it off.

Across the left side of her chest was a wide scar. And she no longer had a breast.

"I don't know if you understood why I refused to accept your T-shirt in the boat. Why I shouted at you. But I couldn't make myself let you see this. To pull off my wet top was just not possible. It's obvious that I wear a prosthesis. I just couldn't let you see it."

I didn't want to see it. But I couldn't take my eyes off the scar. The perfect breast with the pink nipple on one side. And the scar on the other. I wanted to bend down and pull up her dress. Hide what I couldn't tear my eyes from.

"You see, Maria, I was so scared of your pity."

Finally, I was able to lift my eyes and meet hers. There we were, standing in front of each other with no need to say anything. I had no questions. Nothing I could say. And when I finally opened my mouth to speak, Emma put her hand over it.

"Shhh. Don't say anything, Maria. I don't know if I could manage anything right now. I just wanted you to know."

She bent down and picked up her bra and put it back on. Then she pulled up the dress and slipped it on.

"I really do think we should make an effort tonight," she said, and walked to the wardrobe and took out the red dress again. "Both of us."

❧

Pau's door stood open, but he was nowhere to be seen. We could smell fumes from the grill up on his terrace. Emma slowly walked inside and I followed. The large room lay in semidarkness. One of Pau's paintings covered most of the wall in front of us. It had fascinated me ever since the very first time I saw it. It hung, then, in the gallery in Barcelona. The title was *Bressol de tots els blaus*, like the song, "the cradle of all blue." I could see that Emma's eyes were fixed on it. It was impossible to step inside that house and not be overwhelmed by it. It was an oil painting, about two meters high and as wide. And it was blue. Not one color but all imaginable blue tones. As if you could sense all the shades, layer upon layer of darker and lighter coats. And even in that dark room the painting seemed to be lit from inside. I had often thought it seemed to change shape and form in front of my eyes. As if it had a life of its own.

"It's one of Pau's," I said. "But you probably guessed that."

Emma stood in front of the painting, with her back to me. And I briefly wished I had my camera in hand. That I had been able to save the image. Even though I realized I could never have captured the atmosphere of that moment. My sister's slight figure in the white dress against the large blue, shimmering canvas.

Eventually, she turned around, and without making any comment we continued up the stairs.

"There you are! Welcome!" Pau called out from the grill. Then he put down the tongs and gave us each a peck on the cheek. He nodded to the chairs at the table, and we sat down.

"I thought Emma had to try our national dish. So I decided to make a paella. We'll see how it goes. I'm a little rusty. I don't often make such elaborate dishes these days." He smiled and poured us each a glass of cava.

"I hope you'll come back now that you've seen how we live here," he said to Emma.

She smiled. "I hope so, too," she said. But she sent me a quick, tentative glance. I couldn't tell if Pau noticed.

"There is so much more to discover around here. More than you would think at first. That might be true about all places, I suppose. And I'm partial, of course. My family has been here for generations. My grandfather had this house built. Had it built? No, he built it himself, most of it. Sometimes I think I can sense that he comes to visit. As if he wants to make sure I'm looking after it properly."

He returned to check the grill and the large paella pan that he had placed on top. I watched him standing there, barefoot, in his white T-shirt and cotton trousers. He seemed to be completely focused on his task. His hands moved with the same natural confidence as always. On the strings of his guitar. With his paint brushes. Fishing. Cooking. Memories of other evenings here, on this terrace, returned. Happy, relaxed evenings with food and music. Meals that seemed to appear effortlessly. With music and song. And Maya by my side. Another time. A time when Pau and I were different people. We might have looked more or less the same. But we were forever changed.

Pau returned to the table. I felt his eyes on me, and I looked up to meet them.

"It's been a long time since you were here, Maria."

I nodded.

"We've had many good nights up here, haven't we?"

I nodded again, not sure if I would be able to speak without my voice breaking.

"And on your terrace too. It made me so very happy when you moved in. And we began to walk back and forth between our two houses. With Raul and Agnés too. And our other friends."

He fell silent. He turned his head and looked at Emma.

"You do know what happened, don't you?"

Emma nodded.

Pau returned to the grill.

"Would you mind setting the table, please?"

I was grateful for something to do, and I placed the plates and cutlery on the table. But it was quickly done and we sat again in the slightly awkward silence.

"Let me turn on some music," Pau said, and disappeared into the room. After a moment, the music streamed from the loudspeakers behind us. Tango.

"It's tango evening down at the casino," Pau said as he sat down.

We picked from the plates with olives and Padrón peppers, and Pau topped up our glasses.

"We could go down after dinner. Watch the old couples dance. Perhaps dance too?"

"Not me," Emma said, with a short laugh. "Never, ever. I can't dance the tango."

"Everybody can dance the tango," Pau said. "You're born with it. Just listen to the music and let it transport you. Just follow."

"I don't think it's that easy."

Emma was beautiful. That special fairylike, fragile quality she possessed. That she had from Mother. And Anna had it too. The blonde hair shone in the light from the fittings on the wall behind her. The white dress brought out the slight tan. The only jewelry she wore was a pair of white pearl earrings.

"But you know how to, don't you, Maria?"

I shook my head. "Not anymore."

Pau said nothing further.

"Tell me a little about your paintings," Emma said. I wasn't sure if she was purposely trying to relieve the obvious awkwardness that had suddenly settled on us or if she was just genuinely interested.

"What would you like to know?" Pau smiled. "I don't really have much to say about them. I just paint them."

"The one in the hallway downstairs is absolutely . . ." Emma made a futile gesture with her hands.

"There you go. It's not that easy to know what to say. I think it suffices to look. Absorb what you can. I don't like to try to explain what I had in mind with my paintings. I might know what I wanted to express. And I certainly know what they mean to me. How I felt when I painted them. But if my works have a different effect on other people, I really don't mind. All that matters is that they have an effect at all. That the observer is touched by them in some way. Apart from that, there is no right or wrong way to see my paintings."

He stood up and went to collect the paella pan. The smell was wonderful, and I realized I was hungry. Before sitting down, he served Emma and me a generous portion each.

The rice was perfectly cooked, slightly burned at the base and golden yellow from the saffron. On top there were pieces of fish, mussels, cuttlefish, sausage, and chicken.

"I would like to apologize for my behavior yesterday." Emma put down her cutlery and looked at Pau.

"There is nothing to apologize for." Pau smiled again and stretched out his hand and placed it over Emma's. "Nothing at all."

"Yes, there is. And I'm so very sorry. I just didn't think. And I destroyed such a wonderful day."

"I had a perfect day, Emma. Truly. It's been a long time since I took out the boat. Your visit finally made me do it. Really, I'm just grateful."

But Emma still looked upset.

"I'm the one who should apologize, Emma. I started the whole thing when I jumped overboard. My fault. But let's forget it now." I raised my glass and toasted.

We took our time. Savored the food. I'm not sure how, but Pau managed to move the conversation to entirely different matters. He talked about his childhood. About his grandfather and other eccentric ancestors. About the fishing that had been their livelihood. After a moment, I forgot everything else and listened attentively. And I could see and hear how much Pau loved this place. I realized how firmly anchored he was here. In his house. Where his family had lived for generations. And I felt more and more strongly how new and how fleeting my own relationship with this place really was. My roots were superficial and fragile. But they were the only roots I had ever grown anywhere.

When we had finished the meal, Pau disappeared downstairs with the dishes. He returned with fruit and cheese. He topped up our glasses and asked if we would like to come inside and see his studio. We followed him, and he turned on the light and the room came to life. The walls were completely covered with paintings and in the center was an easel with a canvas covered with a cloth. I looked inquiringly at Pau, but he didn't seem to notice. He made no sign of intending to show the painting. Instead, he began to talk.

"It was my mother who made me paint. She was artistic, and I think my interest made her happy." Pau's figure cast a long shadow on the wall behind him. "As I remember it, she was always by my side. At first as a teacher. Later as an active observer. She still sits by my side when I paint. Well, at other times too. I carry her with me always." He smiled. "My father, on the other hand, had in mind for me to study. That I was to do what had been denied him. I think he wanted me to become a lawyer. Or an accountant. Something that would make me financially independent. He was given a position in my grandfather's construction business when he married my mother. I don't think he ever felt quite free, even though he did well and the firm prospered. He took over when grandfather died. Well, it really was my mother who inherited it. She was an only child. Then my sister, Laura, took over when my father died. Not me. The only time I ever heard them discuss the matter, my mother pointed out that she was the one who had inherited the company, and that it was very suitable that her daughter took over."

Pau looked pensive.

"When you are a child, you have no perspective on your parents. They are just Mother and Father. You can't imagine them being different from how they are. Not until you are an adult, if then, can you see them as individuals. And when I consider my parents now, I understand how much they must have loved each other in order to manage to live as they did. I understand how hard it must have been for a proud man like my father to work under his father-in-law. It must have been like a lifelong apprenticeship. A whole life of proving to your in-laws that you were worthy of their cherished daughter, their only child. But I do think he thought it was worth it."

I glanced at Emma, and she looked as if she was listening attentively. Her eyes were fixed on Pau.

I swallowed again and again, unable to speak. Finally, I excused myself and went downstairs to the bathroom and filled my hands with cold water. Then I placed my cool palms on my cheeks. I saw my reflection in the mirror. The dim light was flattering. Not only had Emma managed to get me into the red dress, but she had also removed the clasp from my hair. I remembered the last time I had worn the dress. And worn my hair hanging loose. Not in this house but up on our own terrace. The very first time we had guests in the house. The evening we celebrated officially becoming a couple. I danced. Laughed. And I felt beautiful. I could see myself in Maya's eyes, and I knew I was beautiful to her.

I lifted the shoulder and tried to take in the smell of the red fabric. I remembered Maya and how she had rested her chin there when we danced. But I smelled nothing at all now.

Pau's story had affected me more than I realized at first. The description of his parent's love touched something sensitive deep inside me. Scratched the thin scab that had formed over the most painful something.

A long life of ceaseless love. Requited love. I couldn't imagine what it would be like to grow up surrounded by it. Or to experience it.

I rested my hands on the washbasin and looked straight into my eyes.

"Couldn't I have had just a little more time?" I whispered. "Time to prove that no sacrifice would have been too great? That my love would have lasted our whole lives?"

I left the bathroom and slowly walked across the room and stood in front of the blue painting. Now I thought I could see Pau as a little boy, with his mother by his side, perhaps with her hand gently against his back as he focused on moving the brush over the canvas. I could see her leaning back on her chair and squinting to see how the entire work looked on the easel. How the two of them, their heads close together, discussed some detail. I imagined Pau's father entering the room and his mother raising her free hand and her husband taking it in his. Then standing behind his son and placing his hand on his son's head.

I looked up at the canvas, where the blue tones merged, deepened, dissolved, and then intensified again. And I understood, as I had never before, that this painting could not have been created without that love that Pau had described. That his art had its origin in the love that had surrounded him all his life.

When I came up the stairs, I stopped on the top step.

Emma and Pau were dancing. They moved softly to the tango music. Their light clothes stood out against the darkness behind them, and it looked almost as if they were stage lit. I watched Emma bend backward, Pau's arm around her waist, and lift a sandal-clad foot against his leg. I stood still, unable to take my eyes off them.

Then I turned and walked quietly down the stairs again and out the front door. The air was cool against my bare arms and legs when I stepped out into the alley. I stopped for a moment and looked up at the sky. It was clear with sparkling stars and a moon that shone with a bright white light. I could still hear the muted tango music behind me as I walked up the stone steps to my house.

I pulled off the dress and returned it to the wardrobe. I stood under the shower for a long time before I went upstairs and made my bed. I sat naked on the sofa, in the dark room, with the box on my lap. My hand quickly found what I was searching for. Maya's little perfume bottle. I pulled out the glass stopper and poured a few drops onto my finger, ran the finger over the base of my throat, behind my ear, and between my legs. Then I slid between the sheets. The fragrance was faint but it still filled the entire room. The entire world.

֍

I woke in the aftermath of an intense orgasm. Without opening my eyes, I tried to hold on to the dream. I had been inside. I had loved. And I had been the loved one as well as the lover. I had watched and had allowed myself to be watched. I had run my hand over the skin of my stomach. And I had felt the excitement of caressing. And of being caressed.

I pulled the sheet over my head and could still smell the faint perfume in the warmth inside. At the same time I felt I was not alone in the room.

When I pulled down the sheet and turned my head, I could make out the silhouette of Emma's body curled up on the other sofa. She lay with her back to me and had pulled up the blanket so her feet lay exposed. She had socks on and for some reason the sight moved me. The impression was that of a small child. The short hair, the narrow back, and sock-clad feet.

I folded away the sheet and snuck across the room and lay down beside my sister. I felt that she woke up, but she didn't move. I stuck my nose into the warm space at the bottom of her neck and stretched out a hand gently to stroke her hair. Then I pulled the blanket over us, and I think we both dozed off. Or perhaps we had never really woken up.

Later I felt Emma move and sit up, and I did the same. We sat looking at each other, a little dazed.

"Don't ever do that again, Maria."

I cocked my head, not understanding.

"Don't ever leave me again."

She sat straight up, her legs crossed. I had a vision of a little nocturnal bird. An owl perhaps.

"I promise."

"Not without letting me know. That's all you need to promise."

"I promise," I repeated. "I just didn't want to intrude. You looked so beautiful up there, dancing."

Emma's short laughter startled me.

"For someone so smart, you are really stupid. Don't you understand anything?" She shook her head.

But she said nothing more, just stood by the sofa, looking down on me.

"This you won't have to share. That's for sure. You may not get it, but this is all yours. Has always been yours. If you could only open your eyes and see it."

Then she turned and disappeared down the stairs.

I pulled on a shirt and a pair of jeans and followed. But Emma had disappeared into her room, and I carried on downstairs to have a shower.

When I returned upstairs, she sat at the table in the patio, as usual, smoking.

"Will you come with me today?"

I nodded.

In the alley she took my arm and stuck it under hers, and we strolled along the quay to the town square and the bakery. On the way back, Emma suddenly stopped.

"How about we take a swim? I know we have no swim-suits, but surely we can jump in wearing our underwear? I can do it now."

I looked at my sister and couldn't resist a smile.

"We surely can!"

Emma was quicker than I and took herself unsteadily across the pebbly beach and into the water. I followed. The water was cool but our skin adjusted soon. We dove. We swam. We floated side by side. Our eyes on the morning sky above.

Let everything stop right now, I thought. But nothing ever stops.

Eventually, we got out and pulled on our clothes and walked back.

⚘

We had finished our coffee and our croissants and lingered at the table. The little red-chested bird was nowhere to be seen, and the sky was clouding over.

"Just a few more hours and I will be on the bus, on my way."

"Oh, right. We were going to see if we could book a taxi. I completely forgot."

"I didn't forget. I changed my mind. I'm not sure why, but I prefer the bus. For some reason it feels more . . . well, normal. As if I'm just going away for a little while. I leave as I arrived. It feels like leaving things a little open. I'm not sure if you understand. To leave in a taxi feels like a flight."

"Oh, perhaps. I'm not sure. But it feels good, leaving things open."

"But it won't work. There is only the early morning bus. So I asked Pau to help book me a taxi to the terminal."

I checked my watch.

"That soon?"

"Yes, I have a train to catch. That's how it has to be."

She looked at me, and I couldn't quite read her expression. A kind of anticipation?

"But you will be back, won't you?"

Then she smiled. "If you invite me."

"Like last time, you mean?"

Now she laughed. "No, not like last time. If you invite me as if you mean it. Then I'll come. But it won't take me two years to respond. I don't have that time."

I nodded.

"Christmas?"

"Maybe."

"With Anna and Jakob?"

"Maybe."

"And then we'll go to Barcelona. And you will see my gallery."

❧

Emma's taxi wasn't a taxi. It was Marcello in his dusty car. He was early and he carried Emma's suitcase up the stairs to the road. Emma and I followed slowly.

"Mother didn't give me much. But she gave me two sisters."

"Me too," said Emma. "I have two sisters, even if only one is walking here beside me." We didn't really say much more. By the car, we held each other. Emma felt so light in my arms.

Marcello closed the door behind Emma, and as they drove off I saw her wave.

❧

When I came back to the house, the girl was already there. I had forgotten she was coming to clean. She was in the kitchen wiping the counters.

"Shall I change the sheets in the bedroom?" she asked, and nodded toward Emma's room.

"Yes, please. My sister just left."

I went upstairs and sat on the terrace. It was cool and the sky was gray. The sea looked dark and uninviting. It was difficult to believe that we had been swimming just a few hours earlier. After a little while, I went inside and pulled the sliding doors closed behind me.

I sat down at the table and opened the laptop.

❦

Pau's door was closed and I could see no light in the house. But I knocked. It took a while before he opened.

Suddenly I had no idea why I had come. Or what to say.

"Emma has left," I said. And I could hear how idiotic it sounded.

But Pau stretched out a hand and pulled me inside. I handed him the bottle of wine that I had brought. He took it and then put his arms around me.

"Would you like something to eat?"

I shook my head.

"I would just like you to sing to me, Pau. About all the blue."

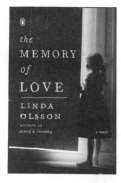

THE MEMORY OF LOVE

Marion has spent years living a quiet life on the coast of New Zealand, a life that allows the door to her past to remain firmly shut. But a chance meeting with a damaged boy, Ika, forces Marion to open the Pandora's box of her memory in this moving tale about redemption and the many forms that love can take.

SONATA FOR MIRIAM

In this haunting novel of loss, love, and human connection, composer Adam Anker embarks on a journey from New Zealand to Poland, and then Sweden, where he not only uncovers his parents' true fate during World War II but also faces the consequences of an impossible choice he made twenty years earlier—a choice that changed his entire life.

ASTRID & VERONIKA

Linda Olsson's stunning debut novel recounts the unusual and unexpected friendship that develops between two women: Veronika, a young writer coming to terms with a recent tragedy, and her reclusive neighbor, Astrid, who offers her comfort in her grief. Set against a haunting Swedish landscape, *Astrid & Veronika* will remain with readers long after its characters' secrets are revealed.

PENGUIN BOOKS

Ready to find your next great read? Let us help. Visit prh.com/nextread